JUST SIX EVENINGS

An IT professional based in Gurgaon, **Tanmay Dubey** is a voracious reader and an avid storyteller. In a career spanning more than ten years, he has been fascinated by several aspects of the corporate world and this book is a result of those observations.

When not busy spinning a yarn, Tanmay can be found reviewing latest Bollywood films on his popular Facebook page 'Tanmay's Movie Adda'. He is also an enthusiastic cyclist, a randonneur, and loves running marathons. He can be reached at tanmay.dubey14@gmail.com and on Twitter (@Tanmay_Dubey).

Praise for the book

'[A] unique and engaging love story with characters very well etched. I enjoyed reading the book.'

—Prakash Jha, film-maker

'I am impressed by [his] deep understanding of human emotions and [his] framing them into a soul-stirring story.'

—Dr Durgesh Mishra (IAS, Retd.), Former Secretary, Government of Chattisgarh

'[His] writing is thought-provoking, simple and yet very entertaining... A new superstar is born!'

—Apoorve Dubey, founder and CEO, Kreyon Systems Pvt. Ltd., author of *The Flight of Ambition*

'It has all the elements of a racy corporate thriller and a beautiful love story. A definite page-turner.'

—Anshuman Bhargava, state editor, *The Hitavada*

'[A]n interesting storyline, and a strong message to youngsters.'

—Dr P.S. Bhadoria, director, SGSITS, Indore

JUST SIX EVENINGS

Tanmay Dubey

RUPA

Published by
Rupa Publications India Pvt. Ltd 2015
7/16, Ansari Road, Daryaganj
New Delhi 110002

Sales Centres:

Allahabad Bengaluru Chennai
Hyderabad Jaipur Kathmandu
Kolkata Mumbai

This is a work of fiction. Names, characters, places and incidents are
either the product of the author's imagination or are used fictitiously and
any resemblance to any actual person, living or dead,
events or locales is entirely coincidental.

ISBN 978-81-2913-681-7

First impression 2015

10 9 8 7 6 5 4 3 2 1

The moral right of the author has been asserted.

Printed at Repro Knowledgecast Limited, India

Be content with what you have;
rejoice in the way things are.
When you realize there is nothing lacking,
the whole world belongs to you.
—Lao Tzu

Contents

Angel and Devil

I

Beginning of the End

22 December 2012
DLF Phase-II, Gurgaon, National Capital Region
8.00 p.m.

THE WINTER IS at its peak in North India. It is a long, perhaps the longest, ride I have taken in my life. I am inside an old van. It seems like the upper body of the vehicle is not in sync with its lower body, and it is this asymmetry that is generating a cacophony. My fellow passengers reek of sweat, dirt and dust. I, on the other hand, reek of the Hugo Boss I had bought during a trip to Singapore. My fellow passengers are all wearing khaki uniforms. The dark grey colour of my suit reflects the colour that could well define my life at this very moment.

The van stops. One of the policemen opens the door. The other grabs my hand firmly and pulls me outside. As I step out of the van, my body goes numb and my head spins. I haven't slept for the past 36 hours. Adding fuel to the fire inside my head are the vodka shots I'd taken last night.

The DLF Phase-II police station is located behind a market. Covered by a four-foot-high boundary wall, there are some old broken bikes kept outside. Bikes seized by the police as stolen items that are never *really* recovered by the people who have lost them.

I have not lost my sense of humour, have I?

The policeman drags me inside. I do not resist. I do not *want to* resist. I have always been a fighter, but at this very moment, I want to be dragged, I want to be controlled. The salesman in me looks for the badge of the policeman dragging me. Shamsher Singh, Sub-Inspector, it reads.

So appropriate.

I have read in many *How to be a Successful Sales Person* type of self-help books that a salesman has to judge the personality of his customer, become a pal to him and sell a product without the latter realizing that he has been fleeced. At this moment, Shamsher Singh is a client.

'Shamsher Sing*hji,* don't drag me... I can walk with you,' I say.

He looks surprised that I have called him by his first name. But then this is the key to starting an effective bit of sales talk. He nods his head slowly, loosens the grip and slows down his pace.

After crossing the main gate, we climb the small stairs that lead to the balcony. Traversing the deserted balcony, we enter the police station. A few curious eyes turn towards me. Today's prisoner is not one of their regular visitors. This is a man in his early 30s, dressed in expensive attire, wearing an expensive perfume.

'*Ke kiya hai tanne* (What have you done)?' Shamsher Singh

asks in his thick Haryanvi accent.

'I have done what I felt was right.'

'Whoever comes here has some reason or the other to justify his or her crime. You young people, the more money you make at a young age, the more complicated your crimes become.'

He takes me to a small room inside the police station. Locker No. 1, it says. The iron gate of the room is loosely bolted. He opens the gate and pushes me inside gently. 'This is your place. The court will decide your fate now.'

Fate. If only I cared for it. The room is dimly lit by a bulb hanging from the ceiling. My eyes scan the room. I see a thin, old man sleeping in one corner. His thick, white beard has ensured that his face cannot be recognized. I choose the other corner of the room to sit. The naked floor beneath me is very cold; I curl my body to grab maximum warmth from my clothing. I slowly lean towards the wall, afraid of its coldness. My head rests backwards; my mind wants me to cry out loud. Not in anguish, but in celebration. For what I have done a few hours ago has relieved me.

2

Catching the Train

'ATUL,' GOLU'S SQUEAKY voice came as soon as I picked up my landline phone.

'Yes.'

'When are you coming?' he checked with me curiously.

'I am leaving in the next five minutes. Catch you in another 15.'

I was getting dressed to reach the railway station. I looked at myself in the mirror of the dressing table in my parents' room. The mirror had greyish spots all over. It was an old dressing table that my father had got in his dowry. His income never really encouraged him to change the furniture in the house. Also, he was a staunch believer of the 'humble living, high thinking' philosophy.

I was wearing a dark blue T-shirt with light blue jeans. I have a decent height, a little less than six feet. I am blessed with a typical Indian brown skin. Not the type girls would call tall, dark and handsome, but I could easily qualify as charming. My attention went to my broad temples and receding hairline. I remembered what the family astrologer had once told my parents: 'Your son has special blessing from goddess Laxmi; he will make good money!'

I found it hard to believe. After completing my graduation in commerce, I had landed a sales job in an electronic retail and distribution shop in Bhopal. I would often look into the mirror and watch my receding hairline. Deeply concerned about my fast depleting sex appeal, I would think, 'Maybe my stars should have blessings from Lord Krishna instead of Goddess Laxmi.'

I was returning to Bhopal after three days of leave, which I had taken to celebrate my parent's twenty-fifth marriage anniversary. I am the only child of my parents, and my father, Alok Shukla, was a state government employee. Sometimes I think the limited income that my father had meant that he could not afford any more children and hence I did not have any siblings.

Like any other Indian middle class family, my parents had also dreamt of my becoming an Indian Administrative Service (IAS) officer or an Indian Institute of Technology (IIT) engineer. But my consistent below-average performance in academics and a couple of failed attempts at the Indian Civil Services exam convinced them that I would not make it to the big league.

The parameters of being called 'successful' for an Indian middle class male are very simple. You either get selected in the Indian Civil Services, or go to an IIT. If neither works out, you join a good MBA college and get a job in a multi-national company (MNC). All the three options increase the rate at which you will be 'priced' or will pay the 'price' of different things in this world. For instance, your marriage advertisement will mention in bold: '**Working in an MNC'**. When you try to rent a place, the property agent or the landlord will ask, 'Working in an MNC?' The doctor will not think twice before recommending an expensive course of treatment for you. Of course, whether you need that treatment or not is a different subject altogether.

Since I could not be an IAS officer or an IIT engineer, my only hope of being declared 'successful' was working in an MNC. But as fate would have it, I failed to secure good marks in India's premier MBA entrance exam. I was disappointed. But Dad patted me on the back and said, 'My son, those who don't make it to IITs or become MBAs also make it big in life. Look at Dhirubhai Ambani, or even for that matter, Shah Rukh Khan.'

Coming to terms with rejection, I began to spend time in the tea stalls outside the government science college in Raipur, and was known as a tapri. I would sit there the whole day sipping tea after tea, and watching girls moving in and out of college.

Gauging the toll that nothingness was taking on my life, my father requested my mother's brother, Pappu Mama, to help me find a job. Pappu Mama ran a small shop, selling electronic items in Raipur. He knew the owner of Tectronics India, which was a decently sized electronic retail shop in Bhopal. It was also the distributor for many small dealers like Pappu Mama in the states of Madhya Pradesh and Chhattisgarh. He requested Mr Bhanot, the owner of the shop, to give me a job.

My family concluded that if I moved out of Raipur, I would get rid of my faltu friends and could start my life afresh. Mr Bhanot obliged my uncle by giving me the job of a 'Sales Executive' taking care of 'inside sales' at a salary of ₹7,500 per month plus a commission on the profit for the product that I would sell from his store. My mother was upset with my newfound job. For her, a salesman was that annoying, good-for-nothing fellow standing outside your door, wearing a tie, smiling and trying to sell you a product you never really wanted to buy. I was not too sure about the job either. But looking at my father's mediocre income, I decided to go ahead.

It's funny how people perceive the sales profession, although the human resources (HR) representative of a company or a sales job advertisement will say, *'It is the most exciting/challenging job'*. But if you ask any student, 'What do you want to become in life?', ninety-nine out of a hundred per cent (I am leaving that one per cent for an occasional maverick) will answer 'Engineer, doctor, scientist, pilot, actor, musician…' and so on. No one will get up and say, 'I want to become a salesman.' Yet most of them willingly or unwillingly end up selling something in some form or the other in life.

I joined Tectronics India in Bhopal and completed a year and a half there. To my friends I had lied that Tectronics was a big corporation and a 'would-be MNC', for I could not have settled for anything less to remain somewhat of a hero in my social life. Ethically, I may have been wrong, but I justified my lie by telling myself that I was only putting words into the dream that Mr Bhanot had of transforming his company into an MNC.

'Dad, just drop me to the Jay Stumbh Chowk. My friends will drop me to the railway station from there,' I requested my father.

'But I can drop you to the station,' he replied.

'Why would you strain yourself waiting for the train to come and then see me off on this summer night? We can bid goodbye from here also.' My father obliged. Sitting behind my dad's scooter, I thought of my friends. We had a *sitting plan* tonight.

Among my friends, there was a principle: 'Never board a night train without a dose of lassi'. This was what we referred to as *Railway ki Saugandh* (the Oath of the Railways). Lassi was a cocktail of beer and whisky, which the group of friends would always arrange whenever any of us had to board a train. This would help catch a good night's sleep in the otherwise hot compartments, the non-AC or the 'second class' compartments as they were commonly referred to.

My father dropped me at the square. I bowed and touched his feet, and waved him goodbye. As I saw him heading homewards, I thought that here was a man who had been working hard for the past twenty-seven years in the same place, working hard for his family, his bosses, and he never lost his cool with anybody. His face always wore a smile. Didn't he ever want to move in big cars, make money and afford other material joys? How could he be so happy and content? I had no answers to these questions. Maybe that's what you call a spiritual way of living.

'Atul,' Golu's sharp voice came from behind. I turned back and saw his grinning face.

'Everything okay?' he asked. I nodded slowly and moved towards him. Golu was my best friend from childhood. He always scored more marks than me. With his talent he could have easily scored good marks in any of the entrance exams but strangely, even after my repeated requests, he did not appear for any.

'Why waste my time and energy in a direction I don't

want to travel?' was his usual reply, followed by 'I am a pukka businessman. I will only invest my time, energy and money where I feel I can get more returns.' Golu's father was a businessman and owned a motorcycle showroom in the city. His plan was to expand his father's business from a motorcycle showroom to a car one.

Most of my friends had either joined their fathers' businesses or opened their own. I was the only 'achiever' among them in the sense that I made them believe I was operating in a corporate environment. Although I pretended to be a corporate dude in front of them and would spin a yarn every now and then to make them believe that their friend was a hot shot achiever, deep down I was ashamed of myself.

We gathered in a small dark room behind a liquor shop. The place was called an ahata. It had small benches with small stools kept in front of them. Guests could sit there and enjoy their drinks. Zero-watt red-coloured bulbs hung at an equal distance on the roof. The smell of spirit filled the air. There were groups of men enjoying their drinks and smoking their bidis. Customers, who bought liquor from the shop, had an option of sitting in the ahata, where the shop owner provided free water and plastic glasses. In this way the product sale was completed by providing a solution to the problem of where to drink.

The lassi was made and all of us quickly gulped some portion of the drink from our glasses. Then raising our half-empty glasses, all my friends screamed, 'Cheers and good luck to our brother.'

I sensed the liquor getting inside my body. The burning sensation travelled from my throat to my chest and dissolved in my stomach. I felt the effect of alcohol in my veins as I tried to take a look at my surroundings; I saw smoke and smelt spirit everywhere.

'Is this the madhushala (bar) the late poet Harivansh Rai Bachchan wrote about?' I finally broke the silence. '*Madiralay jaane ko nikla, kis path jaoon, soch raha main bhola-bhala, raah pakad tu ek chala chal paa jaayega madhushala* (I step out to find a bar, which way should I take…take one road and you shall find your destination).'

'Oye, my Hindi topper, it's time to board the train. Moreover, you are singing the wrong lines,' shouted Golu. All the friends hugged each other. I took my bag and jumped on to the back seat of Golu's bike. He drove crazily towards the railway station.

The Raipur railway station is the biggest railway station in the south-east central railway zone of the Indian Railways. It is not the size of the station that makes it the biggest but the advantage of its being located in a state capital. Everything you have in the city is the biggest and the largest. I was travelling by the Chhattisgarh Express that runs from Bilaspur via Raipur to Bhopal and then finally stops at Amritsar, covering the entire central province of the old British Raj.

We reached the station a little after the expected arrival time of the train. Golu was parking the vehicle, when he shouted, 'You run inside, I am coming after you.' It was peak summer and my T-shirt was half soaked in sweat. With my bag in my hand, I started running towards the platform. I entered the station, and stopped a coolie.

'What is the status of the Chhattisgarh Express?'

An old coolie with an expressionless face mumbled, 'On time.'

I turned my face towards the railway line. To my horror, I saw the train moving at a brisk pace. I started running madly. Fear gripped my mind, but that's what alcohol does to you. It can make you chase a running train and have you believe you can beat it!

'Run, Atul, run!' shouted Golu. I saw my job moving away from me along with the departing train. This was the 'month-end', the most dreaded word for juniors and a revered word for seniors. This is the time of the month when a salesman is expected to amass maximum numbers in revenue and collect the maximum amount of money back from the customers. Good results during this time ensure promotions and the performance of the company fetches a good stock value if it is listed on the stock exchange.

I had requested my boss to give me three days of leave during that crucial time of the month, and not reaching the office on time could wreak havoc. I could not let that happen.

Now. Not now. Yes now. I threw my bag inside the door. A few passengers were standing at the gate to the compartment; the bag hit one of the guys in the stomach. He began hurling abuses at me. I gathered all my aggression and shouted back, 'Get the hell out of my way.' That shout could well have stopped the entire rally of a political party. I gathered myself and jumped inside!

Thud! I landed inside the cabin. The man standing on the gate stepped aside quickly. I clutched the bars of the door. I was breathing heavily and was fully drenched in sweat. More people standing near the gate joined the abusing man and threw more innovative ones at me. They were taken aback by the sudden heroics of a young man. I did not pay any attention to them as the joy of winning over a running train had taken over my mind. I looked back at Golu, who was still running. He held up a small polythene bag full of besan laddoos, the most material form of love an Indian mother gives to her son.

'I will get this sent by courier!' Golu shouted and waved the bag quickly in the air.

I picked up my bag. Everyone was staring at me. The cursing in the compartment grew and I had to reply now. 'Listen I am sorry, I wanted to catch the train badly...' Before I could complete my sentence, the train stopped. I was confused and thought maybe Golu had asked someone to pull the chain so that he could give me the laddoos. I turned back and saw Golu's grinning face. I was contemplating getting out of the train when I heard the announcement, 'Chhattisgarh Express coming from Bilaspur going to Amritsar via Nagpur has reached Raipur.'

'Shit!' I berated myself. I had jumped inside a train coming to the platform and not the one leaving the platform.

3

The Journey

GOLU AND I could not stop laughing. I had made a complete fool of myself. Now that the train had been standing on the station for almost ten minutes, we went to a nearby tap, washed our faces, drank some water and I combed my already thinning hair. I took some deep breaths and was back to normal. Nevertheless my sprinting across the platform and the Tarzan jump had triumphed over the high that the alcohol had offered moments ago.

Both of us went towards the compartment where my seat was reserved.

'Atul Shukla, M 23. That's your name. Your seat number is 16,' said Golu, reading the name from the reservation list that was pasted outside the compartment. 'I always wonder why they mention sex also with the name. It's better to put a photograph. At least you get to see how good-looking your fellow passenger is.'

I looked at him in disgust. I entered the cabin and found my seat. After putting my luggage inside, I came out to say goodbye to Golu.

'I have searched the complete reservation list. No 'item' in the compartment.'

'Shut up, Golu. Now let's part. You are also getting late,' I hugged him.

'Okay, bye, man!'

I shook my head, smiled back at him and entered the compartment. The sequence of events had made me tired. First the heady cocktail of whisky and beer, then the whole 'Tarzan' jump. I wanted to sleep and join office fresh the next day. I sat on my seat. A Bengali family was sitting in front of me. There were three of them: a man, a woman and a boy in his early teens. They all stared at me.

Hey guys, I am not going to kill you.

Feeling awkward, I turned my face towards the window.

'Did you say something?' asked the Bengali man.

'Me? No…not at all,' I replied.

Bugger, can he read thoughts?

I tried very hard to stare outside the window. I was not the kind who liked talking to my fellow passengers. Three minutes later, another lady, possibly in her mid-forties, came and sat on another seat.

This must be Priya F 42.

After some time a man, possibly in his mid-thirties, came in; he seemed to be in a hurry to settle down.

Probably a businessman.

This guy scrutinized his sides and identified his seat on the upper berth. He managed to climb up despite his weight, then placed his small briefcase under his head to make a pillow out of it. Minutes later, everybody could hear him snore.

Must've had an excessive dose of lassi!

The train whistled. I looked around at my fellow passengers.

Dear lord, I can never have a beautiful girl for a co-passenger, can I?

The train had just started moving. 'Excuse me, is it seat no 17?' I turned around and saw a girl in her 20s, wearing a decent grey T-shirt, dark blue jeans, carrying a backpack, hair just a cut above her shoulders, tied loose in a ponytail. She was fair, had big, black expressive eyes, average height and just about the perfect body mass ratio. In all, she was beautiful.

I kept staring at her for a while, my face blank. I could not believe my luck. 'Umm, er, yes it is seat number 17.'

'Okay fine,' she said confidently and sat down alongside me.

Priya F 41? Surely there is a typo.

This night was special. First the dramatic train chase, then this piece of luck. The train was catching speed. Meanwhile, the Bengali man kept staring at us. I stared right back this time, but his perfectly rounded eyes did not express anything.

Plain jealous, eh?

His wife was busy listening to songs on her old Sony Walkman and their bespectacled son had buried his head in a comic book. The lady sitting sideways in the compartment was reading some Hindi women's magazine. I was waiting to start a conversation with my beautiful co-passenger.

'Anyone for food?' the train's pantry man came asking.

'What is the price?' the Bengali man asked.

'Veg: ₹65 and non-veg: ₹100.'

'Huh, what's in the bhej?' the Bengali uncle asked.

'*Chaar chapati, ek* rice, *ek daal, ek paneer,* pickle, curd.'

'What! Only thees much and you are charging *so* much. Is this loot?' the man screamed.

'Listen, Uncle, there is no pantry in this train and we provide the food from other vendors; we do not have control over prices, do you want to order or not?' The man did not say anything; he turned his head towards the window and stared outside. Unperturbed by the conversation, his wife was enjoying her music. The pantry man turned and looked at all of us.

'Would you like to order something?' I asked the young girl sitting right next to me with an enthusiasm that would put even five-star waiters to shame. Amused, she looked at the pantry man first and then turned her head towards me as if to distinguish who among the two of us was providing a greater service to the Indian Railways.

'No, no thanks.'

Had I embarrassed myself? At this point, I suddenly remembered these golden words from a legendary cricketer: *'Once you start with the shot, just go through with its flow. Even if the shot is mistimed, the flow of the shot might help the ball reach the boundary. Do not get stuck midway.'* Enlightened, I decided to take the conversation ahead.

'My name is Atul, Atul Shukla.'

Bond, James Bond.

My hand reached out to greet hers. Stunned, she looked straight into my eyes and we kept looking at each other for some moments. Her big eyelashes went down, and she extended her hand towards mine.

'I am Priya Arya.'

I felt the soft touch of Priya's hand deep in my heart. My face was radiant with childlike joy.

Amid this pinnacle of bliss, the Bengali man interjected. 'All these news reports bhich say railways are in profit are all nonsense. Look at the kondition of this railway station,' his fingers were pointing outside at a dimly lit station that we were crossing. 'And here look at the kondition of this compartment. Bhery dirty, bhery old.' He continued, 'The profit should be distributed to all the employees of the railways and should be brought back into the system to faarther upgrade the phasilities. But no, the minister declares, we made *theese* much profit and all the money...God knows bhere it goes.'

Jeez, this is not an MBA entrance group discussion exercise.

I was in no mood to waste this precious time talking to a middle-aged psycho. By now, Priya had shifted her face towards the window.

She must be shy...she may not be interested...even old sages have said it's not possible to read a woman's mind. Who am I then?

But I wasn't planning to give up.

'You a student or working somewhere?'

'No, I am pursuing an MBA from Indore.' Priya turned around and smiled. There was an inquisitiveness in her eyes as if she was trying to figure out if I was hitting on her.

'Okay, but this train only goes to Bhopal and you want to go to Indore?'

'Actually, I will take a taxi from Bhopal,' she replied.

'Brave girl!'

'And you?' Priya asked.

Carpe diem. Not only is this girl answering my questions, she is even curious about me.

'Well, I work for Tectronics.' I flashed my sales executive card in style and gave it to Priya.

'Is it an MNC?'

There it was: 'MNC', the ultimate barometer of success for

any young guy working in the private sector.

'Well, we are into IT. I mean electronics and stuff. We sell all the equipment of different brands and even send all our products to small resellers across the state. We are kind of an MNC to these small guys.' I almost laughed at my own joke. Priya wasn't impressed. She smiled and carefully kept my card inside her handbag. In the meantime, the Bengali man opened his luggage and started taking out the dinner he had got packed. The entire family joined him in the feast.

What the hell! Why was he yelling at the pantry man when he had brought his own meal?

It was my turn to stare at him.

'Did you say something?' the Bengali man asked with food still stuffed in his mouth.

'Me? No, no not at all.'

The other co-passengers were busy in their own worlds. Bengali 'Uncle' and company, having finished their dinner, had taken it upon themselves to stare at me and Priya. I was uncomfortable and looked outside, but Priya did not look bothered. I tried looking at her from the corner of my eye. Her hair kept falling on her face. I sighed at every innocent attempt she made to hold it back. I desperately wanted to kickstart a conversation this time.

Should it be movies? No, too clichéd.

Should it be hobbies? Aah! This is childish.

I have already checked her destination.

And then voila, I saw a friendship band on her right wrist.

'This band really looks cool. Presented by your... boyfriend?' Amused, Priya looked at me and grinned. Here was a guy she had met a few minutes ago and now he was probing into her personal life.

'Well, this was given to me by my best friend Rakhi. She is a girl...and I don't have a boyfriend.'

'Thank God, you don't have one, and thank God you are straight,' I joked. She shook her head and burst into laughter. At this point, I took comfort in Shah Rukh Khan's tip to all aspiring lovers: *Hassi toh phasi.*

Priya had a lovely smile. I stared at her thin pinkish brown lips. We went on to talk about our respective colleges, backgrounds and favourite haunts in the city. She was also from Raipur. Priya had a working mother and a younger sister. Her father had passed away when she was sixteen. Her mother had got a compensatory job in the state government school. All the three ladies led a modest life. Her parents had had a love marriage; her father was a Kayasth and her mother a Punjabi so both of them were disowned by their respective families. Hence, after Priya's father's death, none of the relatives came forth to offer support to the family. Being the eldest daughter of the family, Priya realized that she had to assume responsibility for the family sooner or later. She had always been a bright student and hoped to find a decent job as soon as she was done with her MBA.

Just when I was about to tell Priya my side of the story, the Bengali man interjected again. 'Sleep now.' The message was loud and clear. I cursed him and stood up with a heavy heart to straighten the berths in the compartment.

As she bade me good night, Priya paused for a few moments. 'I don't know why I told you so many things. I'm usually a reserved person.'

'Maybe you saw a trustworthy friend in me.' Priya gave

me that infectious smile.

After seeing Priya get on her berth, I went to mine. 'I love the Indian Railways,' I mumbled to myself.

A couple of hours had passed. Everyone in the compartment was asleep. I got up to relieve myself, and then reached out for the water bottle kept in my bag. I caught a glance at Priya; she looked even more beautiful now. I thought of touching her, kissing her on the cheeks. I placed my hands slowly on her berth and moved closer to her.

What the hell am I doing?

I held myself back and jumped on to my berth. Did I find her desirable? Or was it the beginning of true love? I did not know.

As I shut my eyes, I thought of my college days. Luck had never been on my side when it came to women. I vividly remembered how I had met Radhika. A tall, dusky beauty, every guy in college pined for her. But she chose me, for reasons best known to her. We began meeting. First in the gardens, then in coffee shops and movie theatres. Soon there came a time when we decided to take our relationship to another level. I borrowed the keys of one of Golu's apartments, and we spent hours there. We became more familiar with each other's bodies, even though we never really explored the deeper sexual aspects.

One day, Radhika popped a question. 'When will we get married?'

'This is infatuation. It's not real love.'

I always thought infatuation was the entry point for lust; love must be something deeper than this. Radhika, though, begged to differ. Yet, when she spoke to any other boy in the college, I would burn with jealousy.

'Why do you talk to other boys?' I once asked her up front.

'Why are you so bothered?' she retorted.

'Because I love you.'

Three years passed, accepting Radhika as the love of my life for two months and then rejecting her as an infatuation for another two. One fine day, she came up to me and said, 'My mother is planning to get me married soon. Why don't you come and talk to her about us?'

How can I do that? I am yet to find a job.

I'd planned to go for higher studies for two years and then settle in a job before taking the plunge. Radhika's family was not prepared to wait for so long. They were hell-bent on getting her married to a rich lad who owned a plastic moulding factory in Bilaspur. Perhaps if my family had intervened, there was a chance that Radhika's parents would wait. But then they were much better-off than us, and I could not find the courage to ask my father to meet her family.

What if they belittled us?

'Maybe this is what fate has decided for us,' I told Radhika. It was the last time she spoke to me. She cried the whole night and got married five days later. I wanted to speak to her on her wedding day but could not muster enough courage. Instead I went to Golu's apartment and we decided to watch *Devdas*. '*Devdas* is a movie one should enjoy with a glass of rum in hand,' Shah Rukh Khan had said famously in one of his interviews. I decided to go ahead with his advice.

Golu bought a bottle of dark rum, and both of us began enjoying the film. The bottle finished faster than the film, and we slept like drunken dogs through what remained of the film.

I remained in the 'Devdas' mode for a year until the MBA

entrance results came out. My name was at the bottom of the table, which meant no decent MBA institute would accept my candidature. *Shocked*. Soon after, Golu informed me that Radhika had given birth to a baby boy. *Devastated*. Finally, I was a 'mamu' in both my personal and professional life.

The train stopped with a jerk and my eyes opened. This morning was beautiful. Perhaps because I saw an opportunity to make a fresh start with Priya. No, I wasn't being naïve. Something told me that we were meant to be together.

The train reached Bhopal station and both Priya and I got down. I helped her with her luggage. 'Thanks,' she smiled at me. I turned my gaze away, fearing she might catch the shame in my eyes because of the previous night's moment of weakness. Both of us started walking towards the exit gate; there were not many people in the station.

'Can I have your mobile number?' I asked.

'I don't have one,' replied Priya.

Is she trying to avoid me?

'Strange, you are going to study alone in a new city and you don't even have a contact number? How will your mom reach you?'

'Don't worry about that, I will manage,' she smiled.

We kept walking. 'Do you have an email address?' This was me being desperate. Her eyes scrutinized mine as though they were saying, 'You will not let me leave without taking my coordinates, will you?'

'It is cutiepie84@hotmail.com.'

How could anyone have such an email address? It sounds as if you're petting a dog.

'That's great! I will mail you then.' There was genuine

happiness in my voice.

As we got out from the gate, I saw a familiar face. It was Rajesh, my immediate senior at Tectronics. Without wasting a moment, I waved to him. 'Hi Rajesh, have you come to pick me up?' I said it aloud so that Priya could think I was in some position of authority at Tectronics, who commanded such authority at work that a fellow employee had to come to the station to pick me up.

'Rajesh Bhaiyya,' Priya's voice came from behind.

'Gudiya, hey, how are you?' Rajesh came towards Priya.

Things fall apart.

I was hitting on a girl who happened to be the sister of my competitor at work.

'You guys are siblings?' I asked, befuddled.

'Rajesh Bhaiyya is my cousin. He has come to drop me to the taxi stand. I will take a taxi to Indore from there.' And then she turned towards Rajesh. 'I didn't know the company you worked in is Tectronics. Atul told me a lot about you guys last evening,' she said innocently.

I smiled nervously and looked at Rajesh. It seemed as if his eyes were inspecting me to see whether I had been naughty with his sister during the journey. Embarrassed, I bade them farewell and hired an auto-rickshaw back to my rented apartment.

How would Priya describe our interaction to Rajesh?

4

Dil Chahta Hai

I REACHED MY RENTED apartment, which was on the first floor of a four-storeyed building. It was still early hours of the day and I did not expect my roommates to be up so soon. There were three of us—me, Ramakant Murthy and Lovely Chaddha. Lovely and I worked at the same place; he was a technician, a real good one. Ramakant, also a technician, worked for a telecom company. I was the only sales guy and would often be at the receiving end of their poor 'salesman jokes' whenever the three of us sat down for some beer.

Lovely had been living alone in this apartment. When I met him at work, we immediately struck a chord, and I moved in with him. Later, a common friend introduced us to Ramakant, who became our third partner. The three of us bonded instantly and began to live together.

Our friends called our apartment a dhaba. Be it watching cricket matches, boozing, or any new joinee in office looking for a temporary room, it was a place that accommodated everything and everyone. We did not have much furniture. However, there was a television, a refrigerator and a couple of mattresses and plastic chairs laid around in the rooms with some essential utensils.

I opened the door with my set of keys and entered quietly and kept the baggage in my room. There were two other rooms for Ramakant and Lovely and a common room. We never stayed in our respective rooms. Like cavemen, we ate, slept and drank in the common room.

I was still unpacking when I heard Ramakant's voice.

'Good morning.'

'Morning,' I replied.

'How was the celebration back home?' he asked.

'It went well,' I replied.

'Some day I want to visit your hometown. I want to see this part of India as much as possible till such time that I am here,' said Ramakant.

'Till the time you are here? What happened, sonny boy? Some tussle at office?' I was surprised to hear this. Ramakant had been in Bhopal for only a year and a half.

'Kaisa ajab ye safar hai, socho to harek hi bekhabar hai, kisko jaana kidhar hai (Strange this journey of life is, no one knows where one has to go).' Ramakant was humming a song from the movie *Dil Chahta Hai*. I shook my head and went to the bathroom.

Ramakant Murthy was a tall, thin, dark Telugu Brahmin. His moustache, cut in a traditional style, and curly hair was a giveaway that he belonged to the southern part of India. Born in a small Andhra town, he was brought up in Jamshedpur. Ramakant was a rare combination of south India meeting east India. His religious and strong middle class upbringing did not allow him to be naturally aggressive, but at his workplace if someone tried to be a smart aleck, he would put them in their place. This was also a reason for his adapting easily to life in this central Indian state and everybody in his office rated him very high.

Ramakant had a very curious spiritual and philosophical approach towards life. Before I understood the real reason behind it, I had thought that maybe he was born in the erstwhile great state of Magadh, the land of Buddha and Chanakya. This young boy might have imbibed the energy of that place and hence had an 'upward inclination'.

Ramakant once asked me what 'upward inclination' was. I explained to him that the 'leftist' inclination was related to being a communist and opposite to this was the 'rightist' inclination, which meant being a simple, God-fearing man, and since Ramakant was neither of the two, and most of his philosophical talk was beyond our comprehension, I used the word 'upward inclination' to describe him. To this, all he offered was a gentle smile.

He was the eldest among us, and would always say, 'I have seen a lot in my life. Before working here I had my own business of assembling computers. It was going well but some financial mismanagement ruined it. This happens with most small start-up business units: a couple of mistakes here and there, and you are dead.' His parents were against the idea of his taking up a job in Bhopal, which they feared was still ruled by the poisonous gas of the infamous Bhopal gas tragedy. They wanted him to join his elder brother's business in the US, but the young man wanted to stand on his own feet. So he came and joined a telecom company in Bhopal.

By the time I came out from the bathroom, Lovely had also got up.

Lovely Chaddha. A suitable name for a big, burly sardar. But he was anything but a big, burly sardar. He was thin, short, had a maroon complexion, a dark moustache, small eyes and a pointed nose. He did not wear a turban and was a chain smoker. He was our 'style bhai'. He would start the month smoking Marlboro and by the end of the month, he would have downgraded to Bristol.

Drinking in a bar was a leisure we could afford only once or twice a month. Lovely, on the other hand, would save money for weeks only to splurge on drinking. Often, after saving money for months, whenever the three of us went to a restaurant, Lovely would order an expensive chicken delicacy. That, too, a full plate. After taking a bite or two, Lovely would say, *'Yaar, dil nahin kar raha.'* And we would burn a hole in our pockets just because he did not have the appetite for an entire plate of the chicken dish.

Lovely was from Ludhiana and had a young sister and a widowed mother. His father was in the army and had been posted in Jammu and Kashmir when an unknown bullet from one of the militants hit him on the head. His dead body was returned home when Lovely was still in college. He wanted to join the army but his family was against the idea. Having always had an interest in technology, he got a job in our company and came far off to this land. But he was never content and would often say, 'I cannot relate to this place.' Lovely always longed for Punjab. He made long distance calls to his family in Ludhiana after the official 'cheap rates' time of 10 p.m. at night. He would chat with them for hours and then pay the huge STD bills from his modest salary. He once told me that he had been saving money for his sister's marriage and had taken a few personal loans from a bank and some cash from Ramakant.

'You say you want to save money for your sister's marriage but the rate at which you spend it will not help the cause,' I once told him.

'C'mon man, what's life without style? Everything will be all right,' he replied with a grin.

All right? How?

Lovely was also a friend's friend. Our fondest memory? Once a promotional event was organized by Ramakant's company at a five-star hotel in the city. They had invited a famous French music band to entertain their customers with live music, drinks and dinner. We managed to sneak in, pretending to be customers, thanks to Ramakant. There was a free flow of beer and food. We sat in one corner, enjoying every bit of both. Ramakant kept visiting our table on the pretext of taking care of his 'customers' and chatted with us.

At the end of the evening, Ramakant came to our table. He was upset. He told us that he had not got a good appraisal from his manager and that his salary hike was negligible. While I was trying to calm him down, Lovely kept staring at him with unmistakable anger. Finally, he stood up and started walking towards the table where Ramakant's boss was sitting. I saw him introducing himself to Mr Bansal and shaking hands with him. Sensing trouble, Ramakant and I followed Lovely.

'Chaddhaji, it's too late. Let's go now,' I said.

'Wait, I have to discuss a very important thing with Mr Bansal,' Lovely blabbered.

'Oh, leave it. We will do it another day. Let him have his

food. He has been busy all evening,' I insisted.

'No, no, sir. Let him say. Is there anything we missed this evening?' Bansal asked without knowing the intensity of the storm that was to hit him soon.

'Wait!' Lovely literally shouted. 'Ramakant, has he given you a bad ranking?' Ramakant's eyes widened. His face had embarrassment, denial, anger, all painted into one.

'Mr Chaddha, *tussi bhi, kinni beer khatam kar ditti* (How much have you had to drink)?' I tried to save the situation with my broken Punjabi and began pushing Lovely towards the exit. By now, he was unstoppable. 'Ramakant, tell me. I will hit this paunchy on his buttocks so hard that he will never give a bad rating to my hardworking friend.'

Bansal could not believe what was happening. By the time I had dragged Lovely out, he was all over the place. That very moment this thin Punjabi lad was ready to tear apart anybody who hurt his friend.

'*Oye* Ramakant *sadda bhai hai* (Ramakant is our friend)!' he kept saying repeatedly.

Expectedly, Ramakant had a tough time explaining his friend's conduct to Bansal the next day. But he never complained. Instead he hugged us when he came back the next evening after managing to save his job. We all burst into laughter. The three of us were as different as can be. Yet we were inseparable. We called ourselves the *Dil Chahta Hai* gang and often argued about who was the closest to the character played by Saif Ali Khan.

5

The Friendship

TECTRONICS HAD A staff of 30 employees and a total turnover of around ₹40 crore. With the kind of revenues it was generating, it was a decently sized company. My sales skills, which came sort of naturally to me, had earned me a good reputation among the customers. Most of them were walk-ins, and I converted them to close deals very easily. In the sales dictionary, the customer who may or may not buy is called a 'Cold Prospect', while one who is most likely to buy is called a 'Hot Prospect'. I was known to convert most of the cold prospects into hot leads and so my name always figured on top of the dashboard that displayed the sales performance of various salesmen in the company.

I was known to have effective people management skills. I could easily become a son, younger brother, friend or technology consultant to my customers. Women were easy to convince; whatever I said about the product, they believed me and put their money on it. I had earned a decent incentive in the last one and a half years of work. The speed at which I was progressing impressed some, while I was envied by others. Not one to give a damn about what others thought of me, I was focused on earning enough money to buy a new bike at the earliest. Since I had no vehicle of my own, I was given the role of a showroom sales guy.

I reached office and settled down on my desk. I was arranging brochures of products when I saw Rajesh entering the office. His face was blank, as dead as ever. He looked at me briefly and I gave him a nervous smile and wished him good morning. He did not pay any attention and instead, moved towards his desk.

Has Priya told Rajesh something about me?

'Hi, champ,' a girl's voice came from behind me.

It was Charu Sinha. She was short, thin and had sharp features. She had a round face, which glowed every time she smiled. Charu was our front desk operator and we nicknamed her 'Good Morning, Tectronics' or GMT in short.

'Hey Charu. Looking cool today.' I looked at the loose, ill-fitting salwar kurta she was wearing.

'Oh, thanks,' she smiled. 'How was your home visit? What was it for? Your marriage?'

'No way, it was my mom and dad's twenty-fifth marriage anniversary celebration.'

'Marriage, wow, what a lovely institution! By the way, when are *you* planning to get married?'

I always felt she had a secret crush on me.

'I have still not found my type,' I replied.

'My type...what an old dialogue!' she chuckled.

I started pretending that I was busy. Lovely had once confided in me that he was in 'true love' with Charu. She, on the other hand, had told him they were 'just good friends'. The telephone at the reception rang. She ran to pick it up. 'Good morning, Tectronics.'

I deliberately avoided speaking to Rajesh that day. I kept myself busy with the steady flow of customers coming in. Being part of the 'inside' sales team meant that I had to report to Rajesh, who was the sales head for Tectronics. I kept thinking of Priya the whole day. I desperately wanted to hear her voice, but I did not have her number. And though I had her email address, what I did not have was a real reason to write to her.

My day ended quickly. It had been a good one sales wise. I had successfully up-sold a fully automatic washing machine to a lady who had come to buy a semi-automatic washing machine. Meanwhile, Lovely had returned from the 'field'. He called me to the parking area for a quick sutta break. We saw Charu coming out of the office. It was 6 p.m., and being a female employee she could pack her bags and leave for home. It was, of course, a sin for male employees to do so.

Charu came towards us and smiled at Lovely. 'I won the bet today,' she said. Lovely returned the gesture, buried in the agony of losing a bet. Charu then looked at me. 'Lovely and I had a bet that Rajesh will not smile today in the office, and he has not done so. Atul will confirm this.'

'Y-Yes…' I said hesitantly, wondering if Rajesh had actually smiled all day.

'Yeah, this is third time in a row. Lovely, you will take me to the coffee shop this time,' she said with childlike enthusiasm. Meanwhile, Lovely's gaze was fixed on her. He was, expectedly, more than happy taking her out.

'Oh my God, it is so late. I must rush before it becomes

darker. Okay guys, bye, see you tomorrow.' Charu ran towards her scooty. Lovely was planning to buy an expensive gift for her on their so-called 'date'.

'She can still be yours. Keep on trying,' I told him.

'Amen,' Lovely sighed

We went back to the office and pretended to be working for a while. Around 7.30 p.m., we left for our apartment. On the way we stopped at Shahpura Lake. There was greenery all around it. The evenings here were particularly beautiful with a cool breeze blowing. With a beer bottle in hand, it was the perfect place to hang out. We bought a few cans from a nearby shop and walked towards one lonely corner of the lake. I told Lovely about Priya, censoring parts that would have him believe that I was a sexual predator.

He suggested that I should take some valuable advice from Ramakant. It was protocol among the three of us; whenever we had doubts about something, we would discuss and seek each other's help. We asked Ramakant to come to the lakeside and get some more beers. For snacks, we bought some roasted corn from a roadside vendor.

Ramakant reached with the essentials in half an hour. After matching our level of 'beer consciousness', Ramakant tilted his head and began thinking.

'You told me she is doing an MBA and is looking for industrial training,' Ramakant said.

'Yes and she was sounding pretty desperate for that,' I replied.

'Hmmm. A friend of mine at work is in the project department. I can ask him to arrange for industrial training for the student. I have helped him with his projects before, and

I don't think he will say no to me.'

'You send an email to the girl tomorrow, and tell her that you have arranged for the industrial training for a week. Ask her to send you an application with her preferred dates. Once we receive this letter, you can call her after two days and confirm. She will be in this city for six days, and you will have those many days to win her,' Ramakant said.

'I will not take six days. *Just six evenings,* my dear friend.'

6

Guruji

I'D SPENT MUCH of the previous night contemplating what to write to Priya. How would she respond to the mail? Will she come? I was gripped by a sense of excitement. I shared my feelings with Ramakant. 'This is the bliss you feel when you are connected with someone in the real sense; when you are in love, you are closest to the person at that moment,' he said.

I never fully understood Ramakant's brand of spirituality, but I enjoyed listening to him.

'How can you think and talk like this?' I asked him.

'Hmm, this is because I am blessed by Guruji,' Ramakant's eyes radiated peace and tranquillity.

'Your Guruji sounds interesting. Can I meet him?' I asked.

'It's not we who can meet him, it's he who decides who can meet him,' replied Ramakant.

I did not understand much of what Ramakant said. I stuffed my mouth with some aloo paratha and came to office riding with Lovely the next day. The office had its fair share of hustle and bustle; it was the last day of the month and the rule of the game was 'no sales guy should be seen in the office during the month-end'. Rajesh was giving commands to his brigade who would go in different directions and collect the maximum possible money and book the maximum possible orders. I headed straight towards my work station, praying no one would ask for my help.

I quietly kept my head buried in the monitor of my PC, pretending I was preparing some quotations and luckily for me, Rajesh did not call me either. After a lot of ifs and buts, I finally signed off on the final draft of the mail I was to send Priya.

Hi Priya,

It's me, Atul. Hope you remember me. We met on the train. Oh, I am becoming so textbook type. Well, hope you have started your studies. I remember you mentioning that you were looking for industrial training for your MBA course. Luckily, I have a friend in this leading telecom company and his team is looking for an MBA fresher for on-job training. I have already told them about you, and he has asked for your CV. If you are interested, you may forward your CV to me. I sincerely think you should not miss this opportunity. Best of luck and take care,

Bye!
Atul ☺

I re-read the email a couple of times, and called up Ramakant to get it checked. He stamped his approval. I took a deep breath and pressed the send button. I left the PC and attended to a customer who was enquiring about split ACs. After half an hour, I came back to the computer, and logged into my email. No reply.

I kept checking my mail with a heavy heart every one hour. By evening when Lovely had come back from the 'field' and asked me if I had heard from her, I told him, 'Not yet'.

'Don't worry, brother. In hostels, girls often don't check mails frequently. She might check tomorrow. Come, let's go for a sutta.' We went outside to the parking place. Lovely took out cigarette from his pocket; it was not a Marlboro.

'What happened? Slipped to the "cheap" brand so early?' I asked.

'Oye, chadd, I am saving. Remember, I have to take Charu on a coffee date, I am planning to give her an expensive, branded gift.' I could not help but smile. After finishing the smoke, I went up to check my mail for one last time. No reply yet. I shut down the PC and came out of the office. I saw Lovely and Charu standing with their respective bikes in the parking. Both seemed to be in a light mood, so I teased them,

'Hi, lovebirds!'

'Shut up!' Charu punched me lightly. 'So how was the day, champ?'

'Yeah, it was okay,' I replied.

'Actually, he was waiting for a BIG order, but unfortunately it did not come today,' Lovely said with his mischievous smile. And before he could say anything else, Charu interjected, 'Okay guys, let me leave before...'

'It gets darker,' we completed the rest of the sentence.

'Shut up'. She drove away in her scooty.

By the time Lovely and I reached home, Ramakant was already there and was talking to someone on the phone. Lovely lit one more cigarette and went inside the kitchen to get a cup of tea. (He had an amazing ability to live on his quota of eight to ten cups of tea with an equal number of cigarettes without eating much in a day). I was sitting in front of the TV when Ramakant came and sat beside me.

'Who were you talking to?' I asked.

'Sir is coming,' Ramakant replied.

'Sir...as in your country head?' Lovely was back with his cup of tea and cigarette.

'My Guruji. We call him 'sir' because he taught us in school,' said Ramakant.

'When is he coming?'

'Tomorrow. He is on his way to Mumbai and will stay here for a night.'

'That's a great coincidence. We were talking about him just this morning.' The excitement in my voice was palpable.

'You should feel lucky, Atul. Many people who are close to him have experienced these great coincidences,' said Ramakant.

'Rama...tell us something more about him.' Lovely also joined us. Ramakant looked at the ceiling and started.

'Guruji's name is Ahmed Ali. He was born to a Christian mother and a Muslim father. When his mother was eight months pregnant, a baba from a passing group of Muslim priests stopped and said to his mother, "The boy will be very special; he will change people's lives."'

'One year after the birth of their son, Mr Shauqat Ali, Ahmed Ali's father, went to Dubai to expand his business. Mr Shauqat Ali married another Muslim woman in Dubai and fathered a son and a daughter. Mr Ali regularly sent money to ensure that his family in India was taken care of. A young Ahmed Ali felt particularly lonely. Ahmed Ali was eight when his father died in a road accident in Dubai. His mother brought him up singlehandedly.'

'Ahmed Ali is God's special person. His approach towards religion is very radical. Since his childhood he has been exposed to different religions. His father was a Muslim, his mother a Christian, and he was brought up in a predominantly Hindu society. His mother's early teachings of God as Allah, Jesus or Krishna as One sowed the seeds of the truth—"all religions lead to one God"—in his mind. There are stories of him reading a book a day. Apparently, there was not a single book left in the city's libraries that he had not read. He was a master in whatever he did. He was a swimming champion, a champion table tennis player. Such was his command over many subjects that the head of the department in his college would come to his house to ask for his advice in personal matters.'

'He is not the usual guru who gives theoretical *gyan* on a devotional channel, but a person with a very realistic approach towards life. I am sure if he starts giving lectures to the masses, with his knowledge and power of comprehension, he can also draw crowds.'

'What is his agenda? And how did you meet him?' I asked Ramakant Murthy. All of a sudden, I wanted to know more about Guruji.

'Guruji was teaching in the same school where I was studying; he was my class teacher. With his powers, he easily spotted what he called "talented people".'

Ramakant smiled gently when he said this. 'His definition of talent is different. According to him, there are some students who are extremely gifted and have a focused mind. They don't need much teaching or coaching in life; even if they don't get guidance they will excel, but their percentage is very small, maybe four to five per cent. And then there are the remaining kids who are full of energy but not fully aware about how to correctly use it. If this energy is not channelized on the correct path, they have equal chances of getting successful and spoiled.

'He says, "A child is brilliant when he or she is born, but as his or her personality begins to develop in a certain way, society starts categorizing him/her as an achiever or loser."'

I now started correlating myself with Guruji's definition of 'talented' people.

Ramakant continued, 'He spotted me in the class. His teaching drew me towards him. His lectures in school were not the usual ones that dealt with textbook questions and answers, but dealt with life as a whole. He once invited me to his home. Once I reached there, I was greeted by a group of fifteen people. I later came to know about the "Friends Club" that these guys had formed. I soon became a part of the club. We would collect a nominal fee from members and use the money to pay the rent for a small one-bedroom apartment. We met every Saturday in this place and discussed and shared our problems, concerns, future life, and other matters. It was a sort of group therapy, which was never possible in any school or college.'

'We would collect money and once we had sufficient funds, we would do a lot of social awareness programmes like groundwater harvesting and child education. We also went out on picnics as part of a team-building exercise. It was a fantastic platform for personality development and everything was monitored by Ahmed Ali himself. The best part was that there was no commercial motive here. We just paid the rent for the place and maintained a small library. I once asked Guruji why he was doing this and he replied, "Out of love."'

I was fascinated by Ramakant's description of his Guruji

and their efforts. To be honest, I felt a little jealous.

'But how can a person be so selfless and do everything out of love?' Lovely asked.

'You know, Lovely, when a person is truly enlightened, he is driven by love. With love, comes gratitude and an individual begins to realize the importance of giving, sharing and teaching. *Guruji* could have also started his "spiritual shop", but instead he decided to help children build their future because if the future of a child is secure, the nation's future will be just as good.'

'Are you guys still continuing with the club?' I asked Ramakant.

'Oh yes, we have opened a full-fledged coaching institute. We give free tuitions to underprivileged children and children with special needs. We charge a very nominal fee. We are also planning to get ourselves registered as a society and then we can carry on the good work on a bigger scale, possibly even open an NGO,' Ramakant replied in excitement.

I was all excited to meet Guruji. 'Can we meet him tomorrow, and will he stay with us?' I asked.

'I have requested him to stay with us,' replied Ramakant.

'Can I be a part of your Friends Club?' I don't know what led me to say this. Lovely was particularly stumped by my interest.

'That will depend on your frequency. Sir always joked, saying one IC (integrated circuit) of my brain is fused,' Ramakant said.

'I am sure that Atul has both his ICs in the head fused,' Lovely Chaddha chipped in.

'You have your whole system corrupted, you smoking bastard.'

This was my turn to give it back. The three of us started to laugh. That night sleep evaded me. I had mixed feelings in my mind; on one hand, I was eagerly waiting for Priya's reply and on the other, curiosity was drawing me closer to 'Guruji'. I did not know when I fell asleep. But when I woke up, I came face-to-face with something special in my life.

7

The Conversation

THE NEXT DAY was a busy one. As usual, customers strolled in and out. The office clutter of pending deliveries of ordered items and arriving shipments kept on ringing in my ears. I was lost in the sea of transactions, a quick lunch and then back to work. One of the senior accountants, Mr Thomas, a Christian Malayali, remarked, 'Why do we work? So that we can earn our daily bread, but look, we don't have time to eat even one slice.'

He expected me to reply to this. I smiled and kept on stuffing the food in my mouth. For me, eating food was not a luxury; in fact, eating food in a luxurious place was. Tectronics was not my aim; this was just a stepping stone. I was waiting for a big break to come my way. The day ended with the disappointment of not hearing back from Priya. I wondered whether she had not checked her mail or had not bothered to reply. I wanted to believe the former.

When Lovely and I reached home, we had completely forgotten that Ramakant's Guruji would be there. We entered the room, and saw Ramakant and Ahmed Ali deep in conversation.

Ahmed Ali was thin, with an oval, clean-shaven face and short hair neatly cropped and parted sideways. He wore light rimmed glasses and was dark. His small, black eyes reflected a great amount of depth. He was dressed in a regular full-sleeved shirt and trousers and looked more like a school teacher than a spiritual guru.

'Hey guys, this is Ali Sir.' Ramakant introduced him.

Lovely quickly went ahead and shook Ali's hands. 'Hello, sir,' he said. Ramakant did not look particularly happy with this; he wanted us to bow and touch his feet. I chose the middle ground. I bowed my head and said, 'Namaste, sir.' Ahmed Ali smiled and replied, 'Namaste.'

There was a certain calmness in his voice. I noticed that his hands were exceptionally long, ending in thin fingers. 'Why don't you guys change and join us for a chat?' Ramakant asked. We quietly obeyed and went to our respective rooms. Later, we came out and sat on the mattress with Ahmed Ali and Ramakant.

'Tell me about yourself one by one,' said Ahmed Ali.

Lovely, as usual, started first. 'My name is Lovely Chaddha. I am from Punjab. I have completed my polytechnic studies from Ludhiana and am presently working as a customer engineer in Tectronics.' There was a certain thrust on the word 'Punjab' whenever Lovely said it.

Ahmed Ali nodded slowly and said, 'Maybe if you can curb your spending habits...that will do well for you.' Lovely was taken aback and he looked at Ramakant with suspicion. Ahmed Ali turned to me and I decided to choose my words carefully.

'I am from Raipur, I completed my graduation in commerce and am working as a sales executive at Tectronics.' Ahmed Ali looked into my eyes and said, 'You are still finding yourself;

a haze surrounds your thoughts and you are in the middle of a journey, on the path to realizing your true self.' He said it all in two lines.

I was surprised and confused. 'Will I ever get a chance to complete the journey?' I asked him.

'With clarity of thoughts and purity at heart, you will reach the place where you should be,' said Ahmed Ali. I could not understand what he meant at that point of time—it was only much later in life that I comprehended what Ahmed Ali had meant then.

Lovely took out a packet of cigarettes and flashed it in style. He looked at Ahmed Ali, asking for permission to smoke. Ahmed Ali smiled and raised his hand, giving a go-ahead. 'Lovely, when you smoke, just do it with complete awareness. Smoke in; smoke out, in, out, like pranayama. Try to gather complete awareness during the act. Slowly, you will realize the uselessness of this and it will not become a habit.' Lovely was visibly shocked. He did not say anything, just nodded his head vigorously.

'Sir, what is life?' This was Lovely's way of sounding smart.

'You have to sit with me continuously for two days and two nights like this and you will come to know what life is.' I wanted to laugh, but Lovely was baffled. Ramakant knew this was Ahmed Ali's way of giving different medicines to different people. Ahmed Ali continued, 'You know, Lovely, most people suffer from a common disease, and it is *sabko jaldi chahiye, sasta chahiye, achcha chahiye aur agar bada ho to aur bhi badhiya* (Everybody wants everything fast, cheap and big). The point I am trying to make is, *what is life* is such a big question that you and I sitting here cannot summarize it in one line. You should be "ready" to receive such an answer and you are not ready right now.'

Lovely was quietly nodding his head.

'What is God?' It was Ramakant's turn to ask a question.

Ahmed Ali once again smiled and said, 'Many scriptures have tried to answer this. Some believe God to be formless, nirakar; some believe God is the Holy Father who controls and guides everything; some believe God is someone who takes a human form or avatar and helps liberate humanity while others believe God is inside everyone and one should find his or her God in oneself.'

'If you examine this from a scientific point of view, we are nothing but carbon bodies breathing oxygen and reproducing. Now if that is the case, how do we classify people like Krishna, Buddha, Jesus, Guru Nanak and Mohammed? They were also human beings like us but you can say they were more evolved human beings and the less evolved people started referring to the more evolved ones as God.'

The three of us were listening silently. His words had moved me deeply.

'Sir...' This was the first time I had called him that.

Ramakant looked at me and smiled. He knew the bug had bitten me, 'When I see people who talk about spirituality and sanyas, my mind gets drawn towards the so-called higher aims in life, but at the same time when I see people moving around in big cars, earning money, with power and women at their disposal, my mind gets carried away. I cannot understand what the correct way of life is.'

'Why should I answer this question?' Ahmed Ali asked with a straight face. I did not expect this. I looked at Ramakant, and he was smiling. I hated him for this...bugger was smiling when

I needed his support. Ahmed Ali read my face and said, 'You know, Atul, as children we always demand something or the other from our parents and this child in us never dies. It keeps on demanding different things from life every time but remember one thing—in life, except for your parents, nobody will give you anything unconditionally. This is a major cause of suffering in us. We expect lots of things from others unconditionally.'

'Now when you ask me questions, let's assume we have a guru–shishya relationship, even then this will mean that there is some form of gurudakshina that has to be given. So if you demand something from life, be prepared to give it back also.'

I was trying to comprehend as much as I could and replied, 'What can I do for you in return?'

Ahmed Ali said with a smile, 'You can give me genuine love.' He placed his hands on my head. I closed my eyes and bowed. He placed his hand on my head once again to bless me. For a second, I felt something in me transforming.

When I opened my eyes, they were wet. Ahmed Ali hugged me. I felt lighter.

'Sir, what is the key to happiness then?' Ramakant interjected again.

Ahmed Ali paused for a second and said, 'You know Ramakant, the key to happiness, if I can put it this way, is to find out the regulator of your desires in yourself. One desire leads to another and then there is no end to it. Desire comes from attachment and attachment leads to suffering or dukh. Try and develop patience and you will be able to create and understand your boundaries, your limitations. You will cultivate an understanding of the boundaries of your achievements and you will be able to live happily. Lao Tzu said something similar.'

There was pin-drop silence in the room. Guruji's wisdom was slowly sinking in our minds. I knew this was just the beginning. I had to go deeper to understand Ahmed Ali, his strange ways of teaching and his equally unique way of looking at life. My question was still unanswered. 'Sir, I am always curious about spirituality. How do we combine spirituality with our materialistic desires?'

'Son, there is a time for everything. You are at a stage in life where you should focus on doing your work with perfection. You can be a paanwala, but if you are doing your work with impeccable dedication and honesty, you are on the right path. This is what I call a modern-day spiritual attitude.'

'I am in sales, sir, and my profession demands that I do *one two ka four* to make it big in life. Look at every other successful industrialist who has built an empire—they would not have achieved so much had they led such simple lives,' I argued.

Ahmed Ali smiled. 'We only see what we want to see, Atul. We don't see what kind of hard work and effort these achievers have put in their work. Whatever we give to this universe comes back to us. Everyone has to pay some cost for everything they achieve. Those people have paid theirs, but we don't see it.'

It was already past midnight and we decided to sleep now, but before Ahmed Ali could get up, I asked, 'Sir...I am confused about sex and love.'

Ahmed Ali looked at me and once again flashed his mystical smile, 'It's natural. Boys your age always are, what's new about this?'

'I can't differentiate when the feeling inside me is lust and when I am in love,' I insisted.

'True love is a very deep spiritual feeling; I don't think you are ready to understand it yet. It's energy, which when it resides below your tummy is sex and when it resides in your heart, is love. You will feel this when you go through it,' Ahmed Ali said while getting up.

Ramakant stood first and touched Ahmed Ali's feet with his head. Lovely then stood up and hugged Ahmed Ali tightly and started crying. I tried to reach out to Lovely, but Ahmed Ali gestured me not to do so. 'Son, I know you are a man of heart,' his hands were patting Lovely's back, 'Your sister will get married to a nice guy and your mother will have no health problems.'

His words gave lot of courage to Lovely; he wiped his face and stood like a small child, bowing his head. Ahmed Ali's presence had increased the bonding among us. We all hugged Ahmed Ali one by one and went to our rooms to sleep. Ramakant gave his room to Ahmed Sir and we three moved into one room to sleep. Lovely crashed on his bed and slept immediately.

'Poor chap, he could not control his emotions today,' said Ramakant.

Before he could say more, I, too, had dozed off.

8

The First Big Win

IT HAD BEEN more than a week since Ahmed Ali had visited us. Our lives had gone back to being mundane. Priya had not replied to my mail and I had almost given up. I often thought about Ahmed Ali and his strange-but-attractive personality. Ramakant had advised me to develop a more personal bond with Guruji. I, too, had promised myself to be in constant touch with him.

It was a Monday. Mr Bhanot, the owner of Tectronics, called me on my extension. It was unusual for him to speak to me directly; he never interfered at the transaction level of the business. I went to his cabin.

'Listen, Atul, there is a tender from the National Hydro Power Limited (NHPL). It is for the supply and installation of CCTV cameras in its offices state-wide. The total worth of this tender is ₹1.75 crore. Since Rajesh is on leave I want you to prepare this tender,' he slid a bunch of papers towards me.

'When is this due, sir?' I asked.

'Today at 4 p.m.,' replied Mr Bhanot.

I looked at my watch; it was 9.45 a.m. Clearly, there was no time to prepare the tender. I grabbed the tender documents as if this was my last chance at redemption. I came out of the cabin and sat down at my workplace. I was trying to comprehend the situation. Here was an order worth ₹1.75 crore for Tectronics and yet nobody seemed very serious about it. Rajesh knew well in advance that this tender was due today and he still took leave. Mr Bhanot was handing over the tender to me on the day it had to be submitted. I had no experience in front-ending tenders. I had always played second fiddle to Rajesh.

Why the hell have I landed in this soup?

Initially I thought of calling Rajesh, but then decided against it. Mr Bhanot had given me the responsibility and this was my chance to prove my worth. After all, for how long could I be a mere showroom sales guy?

I called the accountant's desk to check whether the earnest money deposit (EMD) demand draft (DD) of ₹3.5 lakh for NHPL was ready. EMD money is submitted by a prospective seller to the buyer along with the tender documents to ensure that they are serious bidders. The buyer can forfeit this money in case the seller or the bidder fails to fulfil any of the conditions put across by the buyer in the tender. The accountant replied that the EMD demand draft was ready; in fact, Mr Bhanot had handed over the DD himself to him today morning. *Strange, I thought, for Mr Bhanot to enter this transaction himself.* Putting every distracting thought aside, I focused on getting the work done.

I quickly read the tender to check the deliverables when I heard a 'ping' from my mailbox. I checked my inbox. It was a mail from Priya.

Hi Atul,

Thanks for remembering me. It felt nice to get your mail. I am sending my CV along with the mail; please send this to the concerned people. My exams will be over by 20 July and then I can come for the training. Also, I have attached the CV of my friend Rakhi. Please see if you can help her get the training at the same place. Both the applications are also attached along with the CV.

Thanks and regards,
Priya Arya

I re-read the mail a couple of times. I was too excited to comprehend it initially. I slowly came to a decent pace and checked the date of the exam. It was five days from now, so she must have been busy with preparations and that's why could not respond earlier. She was not coming alone; she was bringing a friend along with her.

I immediately called up Ramakant. He agreed to arrange training for Priya's friend also. I wanted to discuss the mail at length with Ramakant, our chief analyst, but my priorities were different at the moment. I had to 'prove' myself today. I hung up and forwarded the mail to Ramakant. I could sense the excitement running in my blood; today was an important day in my life.

I once again ran through the list of requirements to be filled in the tender. I noted down all of them on one single sheet and started working on each one of them. I checked the delivery department for the last five years' supply orders from the government department; this was required as part of tender documentation to check the credentials of the bidder. I called up the accounts department and asked it to share with me the last five years' balance sheets. Mr Thomas was the chief accountant. He said reluctantly, 'These documents cannot be made available off the shelf. I have lots of work to do, and I cannot to do this.'

I went up to his desk and politely said, 'Thomas Sir, this is first big tender of my life, please support me.' Mr Thomas was childless and he was mostly irritable at work. Every morning I would walk up to his desk with a cup of tea and would chat him up about his native land Kerala, its beauty and our office politics. This was one of my efforts to have a 'cross-vertical relationship' in the company. After his initial resentment, he enjoyed my conversation. Even today, after his initial reluctance, he decided to help me.

Good, this is why I had invested so much time in you.

In the meantime, Charu came to my desk, 'What happened, champ?'

'I am busy, Charu. One tender is due today. We will talk in the evening,' I was neck-deep in work.

'There aren't many calls today. I can help you with the preparation,' said Charu.

I was more than happy to accept her help. I had to make outstation calls to original equipment manufacturers (OEMs) and vendors to get the transfer prices from them. The STD call facility was enabled only on one telephone in the entire office. The phone was kept inside Mr Bhanot's cabin. Anybody wanting to make outstation calls had to seek his approval. Mr Bhanot had moved out of office and had handed over his cabin keys to Mr Thomas and had given a blanket approval to hand over the keys to me whenever I needed them. I made quick calls to the CCTV company representatives, networking vendors, followed by emails to get the prices. Installation was to be completed by Tectronics engineers; hence I did not have to take the prices.

After about two hours and constant follow-ups, I received the prices. Meanwhile, Charu had managed to pull up all the relevant supporting documents needed for the tender. I had prepared the price bid format and had to fill in the prices. This exercise was going to be the trickiest. I took a deep breath and looked at the prices that I had received from vendors. Mr Bhanot had asked me to add 15 per cent on the transfer prices that were received. This 15 per cent was going to be Tectronics's working margin.

I was not sure of the competitiveness of the prices that the vendors had given me; I calculated that if I added my margin to the prices, there was a chance of my price not being the lowest. I then decided to do something that changed the course of the game.

I decided to quote the prices as I had received them. This way, I was reducing the chance of my price bid getting out priced. If my price bid was declared L1 (first in lowest) and I got the contract, I could further negotiate with these vendors and make my margin. There was an obvious risk attached to this strategy; vendors can say 'no' to any additional price discount, yet I decided to go ahead. If a business worth ₹1.75 crore was important to me, it was important to them too. My immediate task was to be the lowest, get the supply order and see it through later. I deliberately avoided calling Rajesh to inform him about this 'forward call' I was going to take; I knew he would say 'no'.

I quietly filled the price bid, took two printouts and kept

one in the record file. It was 3.25 p.m. I had informed Lovely and asked him to be in office by 3.30 p.m. to take me to the NHPL office. He had not reached till now.

'Where the hell are you? The tender submission is at 4 p.m.'

'I am on my way, should reach in the next five minutes,' replied Lovely. I could hear the sound of the wind in the background; I could sense the speed at which Chaddha was driving his bike. I took a couple of deep breaths to calm myself.

In the meantime, Lovely stormed inside. 'Hope you have filled the correct prices in the commercial bid. This is your first one…' I quietly nodded.

I have completely relied on my gut feeling.

Of the many adjectives we associated with him, Lovely 'Rocket' Chaddha figured prominently. Once again, he had to live up to his name. He rode on the roads of Bhopal like crazy—he jumped a couple of traffic signals and as I was sitting at the back, my job was to cover the numberplate with my feet folded backwards. Lovely quickly manoeuvred his bike past moving vehicles and I heard a lot of innovative abuses on the human anatomy both from Lovely and the others driving on the roads.

It was 3.38 p.m. when we had left the office. We were outside the NHPL office by 3.54 p.m. I jumped off the bike and started running towards the building. The office was on the fourth floor. I had exactly six minutes left with me. Lovely shouted, 'You reach the office, I am parking the bike.' I ran towards the lift; it was coming down from the tenth floor. I did not have that much time, so I decided to take the steps. Other sales guys would often rue about the fact that, 'Whatever time you get to prepare for the tender, it always falls short and you run at the last minute.'

Truer words had never been said.

I was breathing heavily when I reached the fourth floor office of NHPL. It was 3.59 p.m. now. I controlled my breath and sighed. I ran towards the 'tender box' kept at the reception. I had to submit my tender before the closing time of 4 p.m., after which the box was to be sealed and no further submissions were allowed.

'You cannot submit the tender…' a voice came from behind. I turned around to find a small, bald man with a paunch, a perfect 'O-pack'. Meanwhile, Lovely had reached the fourth floor. He recognized the guy. 'Shishir, from competition,' he murmured.

'Why? It's still a minute to 4 p.m.,' both Lovely and I chorused.

Shishir pointed with his fat fingers towards the wall clock in the meeting room—it was showing 4.10 p.m. The wall clock was white in colour, encircled by a black thin rim and the two arms of the clock looked like a big moustache of a demon staring at us. By now, the lower part of my body had gone numb.

Lovely sensed that stillness in me and said, 'This is wrong, the clock has erred, even my hand watch is showing 3.59 p.m. It's still not 4 p.m.' He picked the envelope from my hand and before anyone could react, he stuffed it inside the tender box. Shishir was taken aback. So was I. But I still thanked Lovely as his aggression had saved the day for me. Other bidders standing nearby objected to this and a small argument ensued. Before our argument could turn into a brawl, Shuklaji came towards the reception. Shishir immediately went to him and started complaining like a school boy.

Shuklaji was NHPL's purchase manager. With an air of authority, he called all of us inside his room and gave a patient hearing to whatever Shishir and the others had to say. Spitting the paan from his orange mouth, he stared at me. Lovely introduced himself and quickly gave our version of the story. Shuklaji kept moving his head up and down while listening.

'What is your name?' Shuklaji asked, after spitting betel nut juice in the dustbin once again.

'Atul Shukla,' I replied.

His eyes sparkled the moment he heard my name. It was only later I understood why. Shuklaji ordered the peon to take all the envelopes and mark the time that the wall clock showed on ours. 'This tender will be presented in front of the committee. If they decide to open this tender, we will open it, or else we will return it to Tectronics.' I was shocked, but consoled myself thinking I might just have a chance. 'Once we complete the technical evaluation, the commercial bid opening will be seven days from now. We will send a fax to all the technically okayed firms and they can send their representatives to attend the financial bid opening,' Shuklaji said.

He stood up and with a slight gesture of his head, signalled all of us to move out of the room. A gradual murmur erupted in the room when people started moving out. But I was quiet and deliberately kept sitting. Once everyone had left the room, I went near the table where Shuklaji was flipping the pages of a file.

'Thank you, sir. Thank you very much,' I said and knelt down to touch his feet. He pulled his legs aside. '*Arrey nahin bhai* (No, no).' Somewhere this gesture had touched his heart. He smiled and asked me to meet him downstairs after 5.30 p.m.

Patience is a salesman's greatest virtue. One learns to while away time waiting for a customer over a smoke and a cup of tea. This is exactly what Lovely and I did at the tea stall near the NHPL office while waiting for the man who could change my fortune.

Shuklaji came down after about an hour; the stall owner saluted him. He ordered a cup of tea for himself and despite our refusal, ordered for us too. He spent the next ten minutes inquiring about me. His questions ranged from where I had come from to how much I earned each month. There was no reasonable explanation for his curiosity except perhaps that he wanted to know how big my company was. After all, a company is only as big as the salary it pays to its employees.

'Son,' he said and moved his mouth so close to mine that I could smell the half-chewed paan in his mouth. 'Do you want this tender?'

Why else would I spend a day with you without having my lunch, doofus?

'Sure, sir, if your blessings are with me.' Lovely was dumbstruck. He was always in awe of my ability to make uncles, aunts and brothers of my customers.

'Why don't you come to my home tomorrow evening? I want to discuss something important,' Shuklaji moved an inch closer. I nodded my head in agreement.

'Why the hell does this fucker want to call you home?'asked Lovely as we walked towards the bike.

'I don't know, I will explore once I am there,' I replied.

'Maybe his heart slipped when he saw a real chikna (good-looking) guy like you, beware my friend. This type is dangerous. These types can take advantage of a handsome, lone bachelor living in this city,' Lovely said with a mischievous smile.

'Shut up,' I punched Lovely on his shoulders, 'I know how to protect myself, if he tries to do some hanky-panky. I swear

I will press his balls so hard that they will become flat for life,' I replied. By the time Lovely drove me home, I was tired, hungry, excited and completely unaware of what fate had in store for me. Yet, I wanted to celebrate. And all I could think of was a bottle of beer and tandoori chicken.

The Next Morning

I got up late the next morning. The evening before had been spent drinking four bottles of beer and planning a course of action that was, predictably, called 'Just Six Evenings'. I quickly gobbled on parathas and gobhi sabzi that the maid had prepared. On the way to work, my mind was preoccupied with the principles of 'Just Six Evenings'. According to the first phase of the plan, Ramakant was to speak to his team leader about the summer training for MBA students on one of their projects. Since Priya was to come with her friend, Ramakant had to request for an approval for two students.

Ramakant's teamleader, who was in his late 30s, could not say 'no' to the prospect of training two pretty girls for a week. The girls' presence would be a sight for sore eyes in the office and would help maintain the 'ecosystem' in an office otherwise filled with men. All I had to do was to present the summer training in such a way to Priya that she could not refuse it. Ramakant described the process of selling this idea to Priya as kite-flying. You have to hold the string tight enough and loosen it in time; with a little bit of luck and some skill the kite will fly in the sky.

The 'kite-flying' was hovering in my mind when I reached the office and signed the attendance register. I was heading towards my desk when Mr Bhanot stopped me.

'How was yesterday's tender?' the question caught me off guard.

'The kite flew well,' I replied instantly.

'What?' Mr Bhanot was amused.

'I...I mean the tender flew off well. We reached in time and, hopefully. the deal will close,' I replied in haste. Mr Bhanot could sense I was not my usual self. He moved towards his cabin and signalled me to follow him. Cursing the situation I followed him in.

'Have you done the pricing correctly as I had said?' Mr Bhanot asked. I was surprised. First, the guy throws the tender at me, which did not help, and now suddenly had woken up to ask me if I had filled in the prices correctly.

'Yes, sir,' I replied, omitting details about the 'forward call' I had taken.

Oh, please don't ask me anything else or I am dead.

'Well, sir, I had been mapping Mr Shukla who heads the purchase department at NHPL, for two months and have developed a bit of an understanding with him,' I tried to change the course of the discussion. I was taking full advantage of my training as a salesman and giving him an impression that everything was under control because he obviously had no clue about what happens on the 'field'.

'That's good,' replied Mr Bhanot. He was gazing at his desktop screen and without looking at me, moved his head and said, *'Theek hai.* Rajesh will be joining in three days from now. You hand over everything to him. Good show, anyway.' That was a hint for me to get out of his cabin. Once outside, my feelings ranged from surprise to anger. First, Mr Bhanot had thrown me in a pit, and when I had resolved the critical problem, he was literally handing over the credit on a platter to Rajesh. This was my first corporate lesson. I was even more determined to win this tender singlehandedly now.

I came back to my seat with a cup of tea, took a couple of deep breaths and went to my mailbox. I clicked on Priya's mail and began looking for her contact details. I longed to hear her voice. Having looked through her curriculum vitae carefully, I stumbled upon a mobile number written there.

This must be her number; and she told me she did not have one?

I picked up my landline phone and started dialling. After two rings, I hung up in nervousness. Reminding myself of the tenets of Just Six Evenings, I decided to call her again. The phone rang and with each ring, my pulse increased.

'Hello.' It was a girl's voice, but I wasn't sure if it was Priya's. 'Er...hello...is this Priya?' I asked.

'No, who's this?'

'Well, my name is Atul and I want to talk to her regarding her summer training,' I replied with an air of confidence.

'Okay, hold on.'

Butterflies in the stomach.

'Hello,' this time a woman with an exceptionally sweet voice replied. 'Hello, is this Priya?' I was admittedly overjoyed.

'Yes,' she replied.

'Hey Priya, this is Atul. From Bhopal, remember me?' I asked in anticipation.

'Hiiiii...how are you?' There was unmistakable excitement in her voice.

'Great, listen. I have forwarded your CV to a friend of mine who happens to be a team leader in the company; in fact, they are my customers. He has selected your friend and you for the summer training. It is a big telecom company. You can come and join them once you are done with your examinations.'

'Oh, that's so nice of you. I am really grateful for your efforts.' This was the first time Priya had been so expressive with me.

'Ah, don't put the weight of such heavy words on my slender shoulders,' I said nonchalantly.

She laughed gently. 'Rakhi is my best friend; we will come together.'

'Where will you stay in Bhopal?'

'I will stay with Rajesh Bhaiyya's family.'

'I don't know how Rajesh Bhaiyya will react if he comes to know that I have arranged the training.'

'Do not worry, I won't tell him. Rakhi's brother has arranged this training for us. Is that all right?'

'That will be fine.'

Girls and their safety net of making brothers!

'The training starts from next week. Call me when you plan to come so that I can inform them.'

'Thank you so much.'

There was an eerie silence for the next five seconds.

'Can I ask you one thing?' I asked.

'Yes.'

'You said you did not have a mobile. Whose number is this?'

'This is Rakhi's number. I don't have one.' Another round of silence followed. This time Priya took charge. 'I will call you when I reach Bhopal.'

Good way of ending the conversation.

'Okay then, bye.'

'Bye.'

I kept the receiver down and breathed away the excitement for a few seconds. I looked around to see if anyone was observing me. Everybody seemed busy, thankfully. Except Charu.

Did she overhear?

I smiled at her nervously, but she turned her head away from me.

Damn.

I casually walked up to her desk and tried my hand at conversation. 'Hey Charu, thanks for your help yesterday.'

'Oh, so you're getting time now to thank me. I was waiting for your call all day,' she said, seemingly disgusted at my lack of manners.

Such moments, when Charu tried to be a little too familiar with me, were odd. 'Last evening, oh! We were celebrating the tender submission. That's why, I couldn't call you. Boys' thing you know.'

'You and your boys' things,' she pushed me aside and started working on her computer.

I sighed; she had not heard anything. I went back to my desk. Customers had started arriving. I was ready to get back to work, though at the back of my mind was what would transpire between *Shuklaji* and me when we met around 7 in the evening.

As soon as Lovely came back to the office in the evening, he confronted the store manager with some faulty spares in a television set that he had sold to a customer. Apparently, Lovely had had to bear the brunt of the angry buyer and now it was the store manager's turn to bear Lovely's brunt. I did not want to disturb him and took an auto-rickshaw to Shuklaji's house.

Amidst the cool evening breeze, a sense of excitement rushed through my blood. This was the first time in my life that I was stepping outside the office to close a deal. I was nervous about Shuklaji's expectations of me.

Will he ask for money? What will I do then? Should I report it to Bhanot? What if Bhanot laughed at my business sense?

If I didn't cater to Shuklaji's demand, would he get my tender rejected? With this rejection I would lose a golden opportunity of proving my worth.

Immersed in these thoughts, I came to my senses only when the auto-rickshaw stopped in front of Shubhalay Villas. These were three-bedroom duplex bungalows built in a row. I paid the driver and started walking towards Shuklaji's bungalow. I reached the gate and slowly opened it. I walked past a small garden inside the boundary wall, which was reasonably maintained. It was quiet and dark outside. I began wondering if Lovely's prediction of Shuklaji's sexual orientation was true. Brushing aside these thoughts, I rang the doorbell.

'Hmm Atul, how are you?' Shuklaji was wearing a white kurta pyjama. Notably, there was no paan in his mouth this time.

'I am fine, sir.' Shuklaji asked me to come inside. His home was a reflection of a typical Indian middle class person's decor sensibilities. An old sofa set, a TV on a wooden stand, a Ganesha idol in one corner, the fragrance of incense sticks and a huge cloth painting hanging on the wall.

'Come sit. What would you like to have? Tea? Coffee?' asked Shuklaji.

My roomies and I do not drink anything hot served in a cup from a saucepan after seven in the evening.

'Sir, anything would do,' I replied.

'Get us some chai, please,' he ordered loudly. I looked around to see whom he had instructed and I saw two girls peeping from another room's window. 'What does your father do?' asked Shuklaji.

'He works for the state electricity board.'

'Who else is there in your family?'

'I am the only son and my mother is a housewife.'

'What is your educational qualification?'

'I am a commerce graduates, sir. I have enrolled in the MBA distance learning programme.'

What does this interview have to do with the deal?

Mrs Shukla entered the drawing room with two cups of tea and a plate of freshly baked biscuits. She wore a traditional sari with her head covered by the palloo. I got up and touched her feet. After exchanging pleasantries, she left the room. Shuklaji now looked straight into my eyes.

'You know, Atul, this is a tender worth almost 2 crore. Probably the biggest for your firm.'

'Yes, sir, this is,' I replied obediently.

'And I am helping you get this deal; in fact, you will get this deal if *I* want to give it to you.' The insistence on the word 'I' clearly reflected who was meant to be the boss here.

'You will get accolades in office and your firm will earn money, but my dear boy, what will happen to me?' he asked. Sooner or later, I was expecting this question. I was in a fix, but I had to answer him. At that very moment, I let desire take over.

'Sir, you are an elder. I will not let that happen.' I decided to dilly dally on the first step of negotiations. I wanted him to put his cards on the table first. 'I know that...I knew it when

I saw you the first time. You are a talented boy and you will go far in life.'

'Sir, with your blessings I will definitely succeed.' I was doing rather well.

'Listen, I can convince the committee to open your tender,' he said with a mischievous smile. 'How confident are you about your prices?'

'That would be great, sir. I have done my best to ensure that ours is the lowest price bid. I will need your help in convincing the OEMs to get us margins. But assuming that my prices are not the lowest, then what will happen?' I asked innocently.

Shuklaji listened to me and smiled. 'You know, Atul, there are two steps. First, your bid has to be opened and accepted. Then it has to be checked whether yours is the lowest or not. To get the first work done, you will have to commit to a 5 per cent commission on the deal. You know I don't keep the whole money. I have to satisfy the committee members too.'

It has come down to numbers now, old hag.

'Money is not a problems, sir. You help us make a margin and we will take care of the rest.' I played 'blind' and there was no stopping now.

'Hey, hey, hey, Atul. You are like a son to me,' he grinned. 'Leave this money talk—let me get your tender opened first. I have worked in this department long enough to know the means and ways to get you this deal. I will have access to all the commercial bids. I can open all the bids secretly and check the prices. I will tell you if your prices are lower than the others or not. If they are not, you will have to prepare a fresh bid and then I will get your bid replaced. No one in the department will come to know. I can do this only if you are committed.'

I was taken aback. It was scandalous that Shukla could easily turn the tide in my favour.

'That's great. I am in, sir. This will be Tectronics's biggest win till date,' I said in excitement. The biggest advantage of being a winner sales guy is that you become a champion inside the company and also in the job market. Such successes give you visibility among the competition and, more often than not, you end up getting a job offer from them with a handsome salary hike.

I was building castles in the air when it struck me that I might have committed too soon in the negotiations. And now Shuklaji's killer move was about to come.

'You told me you weren't married, right?'

'I am not, sir.'

'Hmm. My elder daughter has done her BA in arts, she can sing very well and is a perfect homemaker. I was looking for someone like you for her—a suitable Brahmin boy. When I saw you yesterday, I knew I had found my guy.'

Shukla was one hell of a smartass. Not only was he earning money out of this tender, he was also getting a husband for his daughter in the process. Clearly, he was the better negotiator among the two of us. I could not believe his audacity. And then I packed a counter-punch.

'Sir, you know you are like a father to me. I will accept whatever you say... My parents are the eldest in the family and they are responsible for arranging my cousin's marriage first. My paternal uncle has not earned enough in his life and so the responsibility of marrying his only daughter has fallen on my father's shoulders. He has decided to get her married first. Once he is through with that responsibility, he will certainly want to see me get married in a well-to-do family like yours.' The fiction of my cousin's wedding, I hoped, would bail me out of my current predicament.

Shukla fell for my lie. He was visibly happy. He called his wife, and this time his daughter also came along. She was introduced to me as Renu. She was not a strikingly beautiful girl. Her hair reeked of oil and she had tied it in a long, thick choti (braid). We exchanged hellos. Shukla wanted us to speak to each other but I was out of words and too exhausted to spin another yarn. After some time, the younger sister came to the living room and introduced herself as Radha. For the next fifteen minutes, she kept on giving me the 'jijaji' look, an expression where a naughty grin meets reverence. I kept smiling nervously through the forty minutes of family interaction. Later, I rushed out of Shukla's home like a damsel in distress.

As I sat in an auto-rickshaw, I looked at my mobile phone, which I had kept on silent mode. There were ten missed calls, five each from Ramakant and Lovely's numbers. I tried to call them back, but my second-hand mobile's battery ran out. I kept the phone back in my pocket. I felt unwell, but perhaps it was my conscience telling me that what I had done was wrong. Not only was this my first professional lie, I had almost sold my soul to the devil. But this was also my first successful business deal that could set the wheel of fortune rolling for me. However, it came at a cost I wasn't sure I was ready to pay.

I tried to justify myself. Had I said no, it would have ensured continuation of an ordinary nine-to-five existence at work. *Nothing succeeds like success*, I told myself. And success of this magnitude would turn me into a star overnight. Shukla would not kill me either; I would stuff enough money in his mouth to keep him shut. Lost in thoughts, I did not realize when I reached my apartment. As I stepped in, I saw Ramakant and Lovely waiting for me. Lovely had his signature cigarette in one hand and a cup of tea in the other. Both asked me where I had been and I lied to them that I had to urgently rush to one of my uncles' homes because of a medical emergency. Till now, I have not been able to decide why I lied to my friends, my brothers. Perhaps I was yet to come to terms with the enormity of the lie. Perhaps I still thought of myself as a perfect human being who could do no wrong. Perhaps. Perhaps. Perhaps.

9

Six Days and Six Evenings

I had been counting days. Shukla had lived up to his promise. He convinced the committee that it was opening the tenders so that they could do the technical evaluation and hence could be objective about it. Interpretation of rules is a double-edged sword, and is often used to one's advantage.

Meanwhile, the first part of the project that I had rechristened 'Just Six Evenings' had gone well. Ramakant had got the confirmation for summer training. As part of the second half of the plan, I had to take Priya out on a date all six evenings. In the third and the final part of the plan, I was to propose to her and ensure that Priya accepted my proposal. Priya was accompanied by her friend Rakhi. I must confess I was mildly irritated at the prospect of hanging out with Priya's friend, but then I decided to bring Ramakant along so that he could keep Rakhi engaged.

I called up Rakhi's number. 'Hello,' she answered mischievously.

'Hi Rakhi, how are you? Just wanted to check if you guys had reached Bhopal.' I was trying to overcome my eagerness.

'Yeah, we came early in the morning.' There was silence for the next ten seconds.

'Where is Priya?' Rakhi, it seemed, was waiting for this question. She handed the phone to Priya.

'Hello,' a gentle reply came from her. Once again I could sense my heart skipping a beat.

'Hi, so all set for training...'

'Yeah.' The reply was disappointingly short.

Perhaps she's trying to avoid any attention at Rajesh's home.

Before she could say anything else, I said, 'I will meet you outside your office today evening.'

After an initial pause, she said, 'Okay.'

I put my phone down happily and started getting ready for work. I went to Ramakant's room only to discover that he was tense. When I asked why, Ramakant seemed hesitant to talk about the problem. I kept prodding him.

'It's a long story and I got a call from my brother in the US.'

'Is everything all right?' I asked.

'Yes, it's all right,' he replied.

'Okay listen, you come and pick me up around 5.30 p.m. We need to go and meet Priya and Rakhi today at 6 p.m. outside her office,' I said.

'Oh, so the lover boy is on the move,' he teased.

I smiled and then left for work. The first person I saw when I reached office was Rajesh, and the first thing he asked for was the NHPL file. I deliberately avoided giving him the file; I was waiting for the commercial opening of the tender, which was due the next day. Shuklaji had not called me in between.

He must have checked the prices in the commercial bid and found mine to be the lowest.

The second phase of 'Just Six Evenings' was about to start.

Ramakant came on time to pick me and we reached Priya's office around 5.55. As I waited breathlessly, a bunch of people marched out of the office, unapologetically relieved from today's prison. Priya and Rakhi came after twenty-five minutes with loads of printouts in their hands. Priya was looking beautiful in her dark brown salwar kurta, a traditional Indian dress, which seemed most appropriate for the first day in office, where opinions are formed on the basis of your appearance.

'Hi, how was the first day?' I started the conversation. I put my hand forth for a hand shake. She extended hers coyly. The soft touch of her hand was magical.

'It was good,' she said. Both of us introduced Ramakant and Rakhi to each other. Quiet hellos came from them.

'Let me show you some beauty of Bhopal,' I came straight to the point. Both the girls giggled and hopped onto a two-wheeler they had borrowed from Rajesh's wife. I piled on Ramakant's bike. Both the drivers, Rakhi and Ramakant, drove side by side. Priya and I kept talking, smiling and stealing sideways glances at each other.

We drove up to a hilltop adjacent to the bada talab (the big lake). It was a lonely place. Parking our bikes on the side of the road, we stepped downwards and reached the top of a big flat rock from where we could see the sun set into the lake. It was a mesmerizing scene; a gigantic orange ball of fire was slowly getting immersed in the water. I slowly moved closer to Priya while Ramakant engaged Rakhi in his ever-so-mystical conversations. We looked like two different pairs out on a romantic date. I kept on looking at her; the reflection of the sunset in her eyes made her look very gorgeous.

'What is your aim in life, Atul?' Priya's question caught me by surprise.

What is it with 'Aim of Life' motto of all pretty, studious girls?

'I don't have an aim. Like any other average person, I want to make it BIG in life, real BIG. But I don't know whether the weight of educational degrees that I carry will land me in a great place. I mean what can you expect from an average commerce degree and a distance learning MBA degree?' I laughed at myself.

'You should not think like this, Atul. You are very special. Have faith in yourself, and I am sure you will make it BIG in life.'

Now that she had asked me, it was sort of my duty to ask her about her plans in life. And I dutifully obliged. My question took her to a different world. While I was candid and careless about my aim; Priya was the exact opposite. Aim in life was like the centre of her world. She took a deep breath, and pointed towards the horizon, 'That is my aim. I want to reach a point where the sky is forced to touch the land. I have promised my dad.' Her eyes went moist.

Seeing her struggle with her vulnerable self, I wanted to embrace her. But I could not dare to do that. Hence I decided to change the mood of the talk by trying to crack a funny line, 'If that is your aim, then let me drive you there. It's only 15 minutes from here.' I pointed towards the small island in the middle of the lake. She made a face and slapped me gently on my hands. We spent a little more than an hour together chatting about our future, eating joints in Raipur and common interests. Ramakant did a good job keeping Rakhi engaged. When the sun had set, we drove back alongside the girls' two-wheeler to ensure their safe escort back to Rajesh's house.

After dropping them a safe distance away from the vicinity of Rajesh's house, we went back to our apartment. We found Lovely Chaddha with his trademark cigarette, tea and phone. Obviously, he was talking to his family in Ludhiana. Seeing us, he cut his conversation short.

'So Mr Bond, how was day one?'

'That was good. Mr X will be under arrest very soon,' I replied.

'*Oye mere sher, chak de phatte* (My friend you rock)!' Lovely said in his thick Punjabi accent. I went to Ramakant's room. He was looking distracted. I asked him if it was about Rakhi, and he told me it had something to do with the conversation he had had with his family earlier in the day.

'Can I help?'

'I will let you know when I need it, Mr Bond.' He held my shoulders and dragged me towards dinner. I literally gobbled my food and went to sleep, eagerly waiting for the next day.

DAY 2

I reached office late the next morning. I had been looking forward to the tender opening of NHPL at 3 in the afternoon and then meeting Priya in the evening. I entered the office around lunch time and headed straight to my desk. I saw Rajesh, Mr Bhanot and his son Saurav. Their gazes were fixed on me. And then suddenly my extension rang. It was Mr Bhanot.

'Come in,' Mr Bhanot ordered in his thick voice. Talking very little was his style. Beaming in confidence, I entered his cabin. He was carrying a paper in his hand. 'Yes sir...' I said

'What happened in NHPL?'

Straight question.

'Sir the tender opening is today at 3 p.m.,' I said.

'Bring the NHPL file.'

Another one liner.

Sensing trouble, my heart began to pound. I went to my desk and brought the file. It had all the details of the prices received from vendors and a copy of the bid. He reviewed the document intensely and immediately understood that I had quoted without any margins. He threw it in front of Rajesh and Saurav. They started evaluating it. I gulped the saliva in my throat.

'What happened, sir?' I asked in a low voice.

'What happened! You stupid son of a bitch!'

Oops!

'The tender opened today at 10 a.m.; we received a fax from their office yesterday evening intimating us about the opening. Rajesh went for the opening today and we are L1. That means we will get the deal,' Mr Bhanot had anger in his eyes.

'That's what we wanted, isn't it? If you are worried about margins, I have planned...' Mr Bhanot cut my words in between.

'That was a "cover bid", damn it. I had taken money from our competitors to submit that bid. I was supposed to lose in this case. Even the EMD was paid by them. I have lost all my credibility in the market.'

Bhanot's words shook me as 'ways of doing business' unfolded in front of me. Rajesh, who was quiet till now, asked, 'Can't we give a regret letter, withdrawing our bid?'

'That would mean surrendering the ₹15 lakh of the EMD amount. This deal is a loss any which way,' replied Bhanot.

I was standing quietly in one corner of the cabin. My sales skills were lying on the table to be dissected in front of Mr Bhanot.

'But Dad, look at the positive side. If we execute this order, it will be the biggest for us in the vertical. We can negotiate with the vendors to get the required margins and we can cover whatever money we have taken from the other party,' Saurav tried to rationalize.

'It's not only about money, Saurav, it's about credibility. All of us, including our so-called competition, mutually exist in the same market. Over the years, I have earned a reputation of being a man of words; it's not the first time that I have entered into such an agreement with the other party. We have also won many contracts by employing similar tactics, and now one rookie has spoiled everything. It's not about one deal; it's going to have a ripple effect.' Bhanot's angry words filled the air.

'Sir, let's think of a strategy to handle this.' Rajesh was rubbing in the balm now.

Mr Bhanot stared at me and this was a signal for me to leave the room. I slowly came out of the cabin. By this time everybody in the office understood that something was wrong. I wanted to cry, my throat felt heavy. My eyes were wet when they met Mr Thomas's.

'I will not ask what happened inside, young man, but this is part and parcel of business. *Ganda hai par dhanda hai yeh* (It's dirty, but its business),' he said, patting my back. The rest of the day passed slowly. I did not speak to anybody and luckily there were not many walk-ins either. The clock struck 6. It was time to call Ramakant.

'Yaar Atul, I am very busy in the evening. Why don't you come over, take my bike and go alone?' Ramakant said.

This was not part of the plan, but has anything in my life ever gone according to plan?

'What happened? Is there something important?' I asked.

'I am expecting a call from my brother in the US. He has given me time in the evening.'

'What's going on between you and your brother? Is something cooking? Your marriage?'

'Ha, ha, nothing of that sort, Atul. I will let you know later.'

'Anyway, you carry on. I will check with Lovely then,' I hung up. Lovely came dot on time. On our way to Priya's office I told him about everything that had happened today.

'Oh bainchod, this is really bad,' he was shocked. We reached Priya's office and waited for some time on our bike. The girls came out talking to each other, deliberately avoiding the glaring eyes of other men in the office. Priya was looking beautiful in her light blue, full-sleeved cotton salwar kurta.

'Hi Priya....' I reached out to her.

'Oh hi...' she gave a surprised reply. 'So, off from office again?' she asked.

'Yes, very much. Actually it was a great day for us; we won a tender worth ₹1.75 crore.' I lied without any hesitation. Lovely looked at me in despair.

'Wow, that's great,' Priya smiled.

'Yeah, I got a lot of praise in my office today.' I continued with my mission to impress her.

'That's really great, congratulations.' She extended her hand for a handshake. I had once again earned an opportunity to touch her. The touch fuelled the burning desire to get her. I held her hand a little longer and kept on smiling.

Telling lies has its advantages. Surely Priya would not have been impressed had I told her the truth.

'Let's go for a ride,' I suggested. She tilted her head and smiled.

We once again drove in pairs and went to Shahpura Lake this time. It was lined by a small garden with not many people around during week days. I had briefed Lovely on his role, so he engaged Rakhi and they went for a walk in the garden.

Priya and I walked towards the railing of the park, which was at the bank of the lake. We stood there in silence for some time, letting our lungs fill with cool air. We could see small fish swimming and hear the sound of ripples hitting the cement structure of the base of the railing. The water seemed to be playing with our thoughts and then throwing them back at us. That moment of silence and stillness had a complete life in it.

'You know, Atul, all this is very difficult for me,' Priya said all of a sudden.

'What is difficult for you?'

'You know what I am talking about, all this, meeting again and again, being friendly,' she replied.

'You are afraid of being friends?' I asked.

'It's not about that, Atul. I cannot afford to do it. I am the eldest in my family. My father passed away when I was very young. Since then life has been very tough for me and my family. I have seen the dark side of this world. You cannot imagine, Atul, what goes through your heart when you lose your father and the rest of the family abandons you. I lost my childhood when my father died. Since then I have been shoulder to shoulder with my mother in every aspect of her life.'

'How can our friendship stop you from doing all that you have been doing till now; in fact, I am very proud of what you have achieved. If you believe in my friendship and have faith in me, I swear I will be your biggest support.' These words came straight from my heart. Silence gripped her. Priya was looking at the deep water, she had also picked up some grass from the ground and her hands were nervously trying to break it one by one.

I kept my hands on her shoulders. Surprisingly, she let me touch her. 'I like you, Priya, and I want you to be my best friend.'

'Are you proposing to me?' she turned and looked straight into my eyes.

'No…I mean yes…no…I am proposing…I mean I want you to be my best friend.'

Shit! I have missed the chance.

She laughed, covering her mouth with her left hand and I watched her like a nerd.

Hassi toh phasi.

By then Lovely and Rakhi were marching towards us. We decided to go to the Indian Coffee House, which was across the road. Indian Coffee House was *the* coffee adda long before Baristas and CCDs were born in this part of the country. Established in the early forties, this chain of restaurants is affordable for coffee-drinking and snack-eating; it's a place where friends and colleagues can hang out for hours, smoking cigarettes, eating South Indian delicacies and discussing topics ranging from films to politics to sports.

We ordered two masala dosas and filter coffee to complement them. It was turning out to be a good ice-breaking date with Priya. As the food was served, we finished it quickly. When the waiter presented the bill to us, we boys took out our wallets to pay.

'You will not pay for us, let's do a contri,' said Priya.

'Come on, this is okay,' I resisted.

I am taking you out on a date, Ma'am.

'No Atul, I don't like anybody, especially a boy, paying for me. We are two equal individuals and we should treat each other accordingly.' She opened her purse and looked at Rakhi gesturing her to take out the money.

'Okay, Madam, as you say.' I divided the total bill among the four of us, and put my portion of the money on the table. 'King' Lovely too obeyed me, although he did not seem too happy doing this.

We came out of the coffee house and decided it was time to leave. Lovely and I drove the ladies back to their home. When we reached our apartment, Ramakant had not reached home.

He is getting late quite often these days.

I joined Lovely in his nightly round of smoking. The faux pas at work had compelled me to think about my future.

'What should I do now?' I asked Lovely.

'Hmm, Bhanot will not leave you easily,' he replied. His words hit me hard. He puffed out the smoke and continued, 'You told me Saurav was praising you when Bhanot was firing away, right?'

'Yes, he was.'

Lovely puffed another one and said, 'Godfather.'

I looked at him for a second and then my face lit up with joy. In Francis Ford Coppola's *Godfather*, Don Corleone's son Michael opposes him in public, and his adversary identifies the chink in the armour.

'Yes, you are right. I should speak to Saurav.'

'I am impressed,' I took a drag of the *sutta* and patted his back. 'King' Lovely was leisurely releasing rings of smoke into the air.

DAY 3

Born with a silver spoon, Saurav Bhanot was quite a brat. He was as old as me, but we had nothing in common. Yet we happened to like each other. Mr Bhanot wanted him to be involved in the company's business but Saurav was never serious about it. This is true of kids who are born in affluent families; they have scant respect for their parents' hard-earned achievements. It is this very arrogance I wanted to capitalize on. Saurav came to office very rarely; he was either smoking marijuana or was dead drunk.

I did not go to office the next day and waited till noon to call up Saurav. He did not pick up the phone. I kept trying again and again.

Still not got up from the late night party, eh?

My phone rang after twenty minutes; it was him.

'Yes.'

'Hi Saurav Sir, Atul Shukla this side,'

'Atul…er…Atul who?'

'Atul Shukla from Tectronics, sir.'

'Atul…oh yes, tell me.'

'I want to speak to you regarding something important. When can I meet you?'

After a prolonged silence, he said, 'Meet me on the highway near the HP petrol pump in one hour.'

'Okay, sir.'

'And yes…don't call me sir.'

'Sure, Saurav.'

I was standing at the petrol pump on the highway when a speeding Honda City stopped in front of me. The window scrolled down and I saw Saurav wearing sunglasses, smiling at me and asking me to sit inside. The AC was blowing on full speed and the car reeked of beer and smoke. Saurav drove me outside the city towards a hilly area and we stopped atop a hill. It looked beautiful from the top; I could see the greenery on the adjacent small hills. The nearby area was a forest and we were all alone there. It looked a bit scary to me. He stepped towards the edge of the cliff and spread his hands in the air.

'Try and feel the air here. It's so fresh, so very cleansing.'

I obeyed. He then took the marijuana joint from his car and we sat down facing the valley beside a huge rock. He lit it and took a drag. 'This is my home,' he said as he exhaled. He went up to the car and switched on its music system. An old Bengali song started playing.

A Punjabi playing Bangla songs?

I was suitably amused. Soon after, he offered me the joint. I did not want to do it, but I had to be his best pal for today. I took a puff; it tasted like herbs and soon a burning sensation gripped me. Saurav sat down on the ground and started humming the song slowly. I also sat down along with him and started tapping to the music without really understanding what was being sung. We did not speak for the next ten minutes, just passed around the joint between us.

'I am very impressed with what you did in the tender.' Saurav broke the silence.

'Oh really? Thank you. But unfortunately Mr Bhanot does not think that way.'

'He does not think "that way" in many matters,' Saurav said.

'My mother is a Bengali and she loves music. I always wanted to be a musician, but my father wanted me to become a businessman, a shrewd one like him,' said Saurav. 'That's why

I come here and sing, make music and do whatever I want to do. You are a good guy, Atul, but Mr Bhanot will not appreciate your aggression.' There was considerable honesty in his words.

I know it.

'What should I do?' I reached out to him.

'Let me think,' he puffed some more ganja and closed his eyes.

Has he passed out?

'I have a friend in Wiretech Insys,' he said, releasing some smoke out from his mouth. Wiretech Insys. It was a big name in the networking industry; they were global leaders in the market of wireless modems, antennae, networking solutions and services. OEMs for big telecom companies. In a nutshell, a *real* MNC.

'How do you know him?' I asked.

'Both of us studied together in school. His father is also a big businessman; his name is Aakash Mehra. He used his good offices with an IAS officer to get a huge business for Wiretech Insys and in the bargain asked the company to get important role for his son. He is a regional manager in the company now; I can recommend you to him.'

I did not know how to react. *Should I kiss his feet?*

I placed my hand on his palm and said, 'Please recommend my name. I will be really grateful.'

'Ah, come on. You need not say all this shit. I saw some real raw talent and aggression in you. You will be wasting it all here...like me.' I could not understand whether he was genuinely helping me, or Lady Luck was smiling on me or was it his way of defying his father?

By now, it was evening and I had to run to meet Priya.

An already drugged Saurav 'dada', as he was lovingly called by his friends, was getting into his evening mood. He had already spoken with a couple of his friends over the phone who were arranging Cuban rum for him. He insisted I join him. 'My mom and dad are coming to Bhopal today and I need to pick them up from the railway station.' I threw yet another lie.

Oh my God, I am getting better at this.

'Ah, then you need to go back to city. Let's drive back and I will show you my way,' he said looking at me with his bloodshot eyes. We sat down in his car and lowered the back rest of the driving seat to an angle where his eyes could see only the edge of the steering. I could not believe this: I was sitting in a car with a drugged moron, who was driving it in his own twisted way. I pretended to be equally thrilled at the prospect of embarking on the adventure that might just have killed both of us.

He dropped me in the city, and I hurriedly boarded an auto-rickshaw. I was late by thirty minutes. I looked at my phone; there were fifteen missed calls from Shuklaji. I had not spoken to him ever since we had met at his house and he was chasing me as a cat would chase a mouse.

Perhaps Rajesh has told him everything.

I wanted to call Priya and ask her to wait for me, but decided against it. I wanted to see if she would wait for me instinctively. The marijuana in my body was making my head spin. I gathered myself and looked around at the parking stand and saw what my eyes wanted to see. Rakhi was sitting on her scooter and Priya was standing with her.

'Hi girls,' I approached them.

'Hi,' both of them said simultaneously.

'Waiting for me?'

'No, waiting for another friend of yours. Today is the third day and we expected another friend of yours,' Rakhi said.

'Don't worry, I have run out of stock,' I joked. Priya was silent.

'Hi Priya,' I said.

'Hi,' she said softly and looked at Rakhi, who, in turn, stopped smiling. 'Atul, let's put an end to all this,' Priya said.

'I don't understand,' I said and looked at Rakhi, who preferred to keep quiet.

'Atul, I am sorry, but I can't have any kind of relationship with you or for that matter with anybody.' Priya chose not to face me but I could see her eyes were moist.

'Rakhi, if you don't mind can I borrow your scooter and take Priya for a ride? We will be back soon.' This was my last resort.

Rakhi looked at Priya, she did not say anything. 'It's okay, you can take the keys and I will wait for you guys.' She took her bag and started walking towards a cyber café. Priya sat behind me and I drove her towards a lonely patch near the bada talab. Priya was careful not to touch me even accidentally.

We reached the place and made ourselves comfortable on cemented seats facing the lake. Priya looked more morose than she had a few moments ago.

'You look more beautiful when your face is sullen,' I tried to break the silence. She smiled gently and turned her head in the other direction. 'Priya, why are you doing this?' The marijuana kick had lent me some confidence.

'Atul, you are a nice guy. I am sure you can get some other good girl,' she pleaded.

'But why can't you be that good girl?'

'My circumstances are different, Atul. I can't be in any relationship. This will be distracting for me. Love and relationships are not my priority. I want to make a career and earn enough money for my mother and sister.'

'What if I say your priority is my priority? What if I say my love will not be a distraction but an inspiration for you? What if I say I will always be standing by you?' Loads of Bollywood films and smoking up had helped me achieve this eloquence. Then in the spur of the moment, I went down on my knees and held her hand. 'I propose to you, Miss Priya Arya. I love you from the bottom of my heart. Do you accept me?'

Priya was taken aback. So was a couple standing at a distance. I was looking straight in Priya's eyes; her face looked clueless and even more beautiful. After a pause of a few seconds, she finally said, 'I need some time to think.'

Must matters of heart be dealt with by the mind?

This was Priya Arya, who always put her mind ahead of her heart. *What would life be with her?* I wondered. *And what would it be without her?* I shuddered. Both of us were silent during our ride back. Rakhi had come back from the cyber café and was waiting for Priya. I said a warm goodbye to her and turned away with a heavy heart. On the way back to my apartment, I called up Ramakant and told him the entire story, including Saurav's gesture of helping me get a new job. He gave it a patient hearing and asked me to take it easy. He hung up saying he had to finish some work and would talk to me the next morning. I reached my apartment and soon found myself lying on my bed.

DAY 4

By the time I got up the next morning, Lovely had already left for office and Ramakant, to my surprise, was waiting for me to get up. He was in his shorts and T-shirt and was working on his old assembled desktop.

'Hi Rama, good morning. Going late to office?' I asked.

'*Nahin re*, I have put in my papers.'

'What the hell! What happened? For the last so many days you had been busy, did you have a fight with your boss?'

I fired many questions at him.

'Nothing of that sort; in fact, I was late every day as I was on call with my elder brother. After a lot of discussion, I have decided to join my elder brother's consultancy firm in the US.'

'Isn't that against your plan in life? You wanted to carve a career of your own? You always had the option of joining him when your business failed, yet you decided to come to Bhopal. What happened to all that gyan?' I was a bit agitated, especially because Rama was planning to leave us and we had no inkling about it.

'*Kahaan kisi ke liye hai mumkin, sabke liye eksah ona, thodasa dil mera bhala hai, thoda bura hai seene mein* (It is not possible to be the same to everyone, my heart is a little good and a little bad),' he sung a line from a Hindi film song.

'Stop that shit. I need an answer,' I wanted him to be logical today.

'I gave it a thought; this was the best decision I could have taken at this moment. Bhai's business is growing; he will do well with some extra pair of hands.'

'Have you discussed this with Guruji?' I asked.

'I always do. He supports my decision.'

'So, our story ends here. Mr Ramakant Murthy, ten years from now you will be a hotshot consultant in the US. Congrats and best of luck,' I stood up.

'Atul,' he also stood up and hugged me, 'I know you are upset, but that's the hard fact of life, change is the only constant,' preached my philosophical friend.

'Okay, my siddha purush (enlightened one), when are you leaving?' I asked.

'Day after tomorrow.'

'Isn't that quite a hush-hush affair?'

'True, I am heading for Delhi. From there, I'll take a flight to the US.'

'That's great.' I paused for a moment, 'I am going to have a telephonic interview with Wiretech Insys today.'

'Saurav is living up to his promise. Do you need any help to prepare?' Ramakant always treated himself as my elder brother.

'Just leave your technical presentation on networking to me.' Ramakant handed over the documents to me; I started reading them but could not focus. I was upset that he was leaving me.

'So Priya said "no"?' asked Ramakant from his room. He was getting ready to go to office to complete the resignation formalities.

'No, she said she needs time to think,' I replied from my room.

Ramakant came to my room and handed over the bike keys to me. 'I am going to office. You will need my bike to take Priya for a ride today. You can pick me up later in the evening and we will celebrate my farewell.'

'I can take a rickshaw,' I tried reasoning with him. 'It's okay, yaar.'

'I don't know if she will accept my proposal or not.' Ramakant was about to leave the room when he stopped.

'She will,' he smiled and left.

I shook my head. Once Ramakant left, I called up Lovely to tell him about the latest development. But he already knew of Rama's decision. Lovely sounded low, but soon came back to his spirits, '*Oye koi nai, yaar*. We will swim in whiskey and beer today and this bugger would remember us forever.' He went on to call some of our other friends for tonight's farewell party for Ramakant.

It wasn't until the afternoon that I got a call from Wiretech Insys HR. After fifteen minutes of the telephonic interview, they put me on a conference call with the hiring manager. Aakash Mehra took my interview for about thirty-five minutes. Since he was Saurav's friend, he did not grill me much by asking any uncomfortable questions. He told me to be present for a video conference call with the vice president of the company the next day at their Bhopal office. He suggested that I be a bit more aggressive during the interview.

Little does he know that I am about to lose my current job thanks to my aggression!

In the evening, I followed my ritual of dressing up and rushing to meet Priya. I was running late because of the interview. *Will she wait or will she leave?* My heart was pounding. When I reached her office, I saw Priya and Rakhi waiting for me in the parking stand.

Thank God!

'Hi,' I tried every bit to conceal my excitement. Rakhi was the first to smile back at me. 'I am not happy with you; you made Priya cry the whole night and she did not sleep for a single minute.' I looked at Priya. She was not looking at me. I could spot dark circles under her big eyes.

'Should we go now?' Priya asked me. I quietly obeyed her and drove her to the same place where I had proposed to her last evening. We strolled towards the railing of the lake.

'Tell me,' I broke the silence. Yet again.

'Tell me what?' she retorted.

'Tell me what I want to hear.'

She turned her head away and tears filled her eyes again.

You need courage to cry so often!

'I could not sleep last night. I kept on contemplating about what I should do. On the one hand I have a career waiting for me, on the other, there's you. I felt with you by my side, I will be stronger and will be able to face any challenges.' I was beginning to expect the unexpected. 'You are a good boy, but I know boys. You will also ditch me,' she said.

I don't know what got to me, but I went down on my knees again and blabbered, 'I commit, Oh My Love, that I shall love you until the end of this world. Do you accept me?'

She burst into laughter, and said, 'I do.'

THIS IS IT!

I got up and held Priya by her shoulders and kissed her gently on her forehead. I wanted to hug her tightly and plant a kiss on her lips, but our surroundings did not allow me to do so. Although there were couples around, public displays of affection were frowned upon in a place like Bhopal. More often than not, you would end up being caught by the police who would make the boy sit in a murga pose and would call the girl's home to tell her parents how their daughter was giving up on Indian culture.

'Let's go home, it's getting late now,' Priya held my hand and dragged me to the bike. Her touch and words had a totally new meaning now. I wanted everything to come to a standstill at this point. Every hurdle seemed surpassable, every goal seemed attainable. We reached the cyber café where Rakhi was waiting for us. She came out smiling.

The girls knew it from the beginning.

Priya waited till Rakhi joined us, 'When is Ramakant leaving?' she asked. It came as a surprise; I had not told her that.

'How do you know that?'

'He came to meet me today, and told me everything about you, your feelings towards me. He helped me pass the final mental hurdle, made me decide,' she replied. 'I am sorry; he did not want me to tell you about his meeting.'

Ramakant! Oh, how badly I wanted to punch him! He hadn't gone straight to his office but had stopped by at Priya's office to tell her how much she meant to me. I wanted to ask her if she had accepted me only because Ramakant had convinced her, but decided against it. Some things in life should just be left untouched.

Meanwhile, Rakhi joined us and it was time to say goodbye. I did not want to leave Priya. She shook my hand and both of us waved goodbye to each other, promising to go for a 'date' tomorrow evening. As I rode back, I had mixed feelings about the situation. I was not able to separate the affection I felt for Priya with the massive boost her acceptance had given to my male ego. She was beautiful and I wanted her. At the same time, I wanted to impress my friends by winning over a beautiful girl. I was happy, but was also beginning to feel scared of committing myself.

With great commitment comes greater responsibility. I wasn't sure if I was ready to be responsible for someone else. I could not foresee where Priya and I would be heading from this point, but that's why love is a crazy journey, isn't it? I picked up Ramakant from his office. He was standing outside with his friends enjoying a drag of sutta at a nearby paan shop. I exchanged pleasantries with his friends, who promised that they would join us in the evening. On the way back, I told Rama that Priya had accepted my proposal and we were 'officially' a couple now.

'Finally, the magic of Mr Bond has worked,' he congratulated me. I gave him a victorious smile. But neither he nor I mentioned that I was aware of his heroics. Being a good friend and a genuine well-wisher, Ramakant didn't think it was right to tell me about his involvement in the matter. We reached home and were greeted by Lovely and a couple of other friends who had joined us for the party. Without wasting any time, we got into our groove by filling our glasses with divine spirits. We 'swam' in alcohol till 2 a.m. Lovely had two more pegs than his normal capacity to celebrate the latest turn of events in my love life.

By the time the last of our guests had left, the three of us were swinging like pendulums and holding each other. And then all of a sudden, tears in my eyes blurred my vision. 'How will we live without you, Rama?' I said, as a tear rolled down my cheek.

'Arrey, don't worry. It's a new beginning for us. You will also get a new job in Delhi, and we all will meet again and celebrate in a five-star hotel.'

'Bastards, you are going to leave me one by one, bainchod. I will also come with you guys,' Lovely Chaddha made a late entry into the conversation and hugged us. The three of us stood and hugged each other for the longest time. If only we had known this would be our last celebration of togetherness.

DAY 5
I got up the next morning to find Ramakant packing his stuff. He was catching a train to Delhi in the afternoon. Since I was not going to office, Lovely had left for work without disturbing me. Now that we were a couple, I called up Priya on Rakhi's phone and she picked up the call.

'Hello.'

'Hi, what are you doing?'

'Jogging! I am in office, baba, preparing my report.'

'Oh, an important report,' I mocked, 'Why don't you skip your office in the second half. Only a day is left. Let's spend some quality time together before you leave.'

I could sense Priya smiling at my insistence on 'quality time'.

'Let me see, I will call you,' she hung up.

I needed to prepare for the interview with the vice president of Wiretech Insys. Ramakant gave me some white papers on wireless technology and I began cramming. I did a mock interview session standing in front of the mirror. I had taken leave from work and was planning not to take any calls from work just when my phone rang and I saw Charu's name flashing on my mobile. I picked it up.

'Hi Atul, long time. Where have you been?' she sounded concerned.

'Nothing, I have a viral fever,' I lied.

'Oh, I thought the scolding that you got from Mr Bhanot kept you away from office.'

Gosh, the whole office now knows of my heroics!

'No, the scolding has nothing to do with my absence. It was just...I was not well. I will join soon. Were Mr Bhanot or Rajesh asking for me?' I straightaway came to the point.

'Ah yes, they were. Two big men in kurta pyjamas came to the office and were inquiring about you. They were sadakchaap, gunda (goon) types,' Charu said hesitatingly.

'What? Who were they? What were they saying?'

'They came and started asking about you, then Rajesh met them and they were referring to some Shuklaji.'

I understood the story. I had not picked up Shukla's phone calls and whenever I did, I made an excuse and hung up. Now, he had sent his boys to terrorize me. 'Did you hear what Rajesh said to them?' I asked her.

'I tried a lot, but I could not hear what they were discussing. Later in the evening I saw Rajesh updating Mr Bhanot about this incident.'

I was even more worried now for two reasons. One, bloodthirsty Shukla's goons were looking for me and second, what if Rajesh told Priya about the entire Shukla episode?

'I am worried about you. Is everything all right?' Charu's words cut through my thoughts.

'Everything is fine, don't worry about me and, yes, a big thank you for your effort.' I was distracted. But the turn of events made me even more determined to crack the Wiretech interview. Lovely came in the afternoon to drop Ramakant to the railway station. Both of us hugged Rama one by one. We made arrangements to 'pack' his bike to be sent to his hometown, Jamshedpur, by train.

Ramakant held me by my shoulders. 'Atul, it's been really

great sharing the last one-and-a-half years of my life with you guys—the joys, the sorrows, the pain and, most importantly, the dreams. I am going after my dream, and so will you one day.'

'Amen,' Lovely said immediately, his face not betraying his sorrow.

'We remain friends forever,' said Ramakant.

'Forever,' Lovely replied.

'Forever...,' I said slowly. Words were not coming out of my throat easily.

'And one more thing, just be in touch with Guruji.' We nodded in affirmation.

Ramakant left on Lovely's bike. I bade him goodbye. Standing alone and walking back to the apartment felt lonelier than ever. The echo in Ramakant's empty room never seemed to leave the place.

While getting ready for the video conference, lost in my thoughts, I went to his room hoping he would, somehow, offer some valuable suggestion like always. Alas, he wasn't there. Finally, I was coming face-to-face with a strange, momentary dullness. I tried to calm myself and wore a light shirt, dark trousers and a matching tie for my much-anticipated interview. Excited and nervous, I took an auto-rickshaw to the Wiretech Insys office.

After an initial connectivity problem, the video conference started. The vice president of Wiretech Insys was Mr Samir Kapoor. He had thick, greyish hair, wore glasses and had a rather prominent moustache. He was smartly dressed in a dark blue business suit. Since he had been in the business for years, he could sense my nervousness and tried to make me feel comfortable by starting off with questions about my family and friends.

Once he had heard what he wanted to, he bombarded me with more profound questions—*Where do you see yourself ten years from now? What are your biggest strengths and weaknesses? What inspires you? Take me through one of your successful sales deals. What do you think a good sales guy should be? Why do you want to leave the current organization?* At the end of the day, these questions were meant to probe the candidate's command over spoken English and diplomatic skills.

Mr Kapoor rounded up the interview with a set of technical questions, the answers to which I had prepared. In the forty-five-minute grilling session, I kept on providing diplomatic answers to his equally diplomatic questions. 'I am done, do you want to ask any questions?' Mr Kapoor sounded like a surgeon who had just operated on a patient.

Yes, how soon will I get the appointment letter?

'It's okay, sir. I don't have any questions,' I replied.

'We will get back to you soon,' said Mr Kapoor with an air of authority.

I felt positive about my performance in the interview and felt a sense of gratitude towards Saurav. I wanted to update him about the interview when my cell phone beeped. It was from Rakhi's phone.

Meet me outside office at 2. Pi.Ya.☺,

I smiled and wrote, OK Ji.

I rushed towards Priya's office. She had bunked her post-lunch session and was waiting for me in the parking. Both of us drove on her two-wheeler towards Kerwa dam. This was a lonely place and a beautiful one too. The dam, although small in size, was built on the bank of a huge lake. We walked on the boundary of the dam for a while and sat on the wall with our legs hanging towards the lake. Both of us were awed by the scenic beauty of the place. Priya was wearing a ring. I took her hand and touched the ring.

'Beautiful, it is.' She smiled and understood my intentions. She let me hold her hand. I moved closer. Our bodies were not touching but I could still smell her perfume.

'I knew you were the one when I saw you first on the train. What did you feel about me?' I was asking a dangerous question.

'I knew you were hitting on me,' she giggled.

'I haven't hit you yet,' I raised my hand. As I brought my hand closer to her cheek pretending to slap her, she closed her eyes. I slowly moved forward and kissed her gently on her soft lips. She moved back immediately.

'What? My lips don't have an electric current running through them,' I said cheekily.

'This is not good, Atul,' Priya said, shifting away from me.

'If you are not comfortable, I won't do it.' It was my turn to shift away from her. We sat silently looking away from each other for some time.

'Did I hurt you?' she asked.

'No,' I said slowly without looking at her. She moved closer to me and with her hand moved my head towards her.

'Do it, if you like it.' She placed her hands on her side as if to surrender herself to me. I smiled and patted her cheeks. 'It's okay.' We looked at each other and then, the very next moment, kissed passionately. Seeing a sense of belongingness and possessiveness in each other's eyes, we hugged each other and kissed a couple of times.

After about half an hour, some labourers working at a nearby construction site passed by. The looks on their faces made us realize that it was time to move away. We decided to go to some other place, and drove to the nearby area.

'We will keep on burning petrol like this,' she said.

'Where can we go now?' I asked. 'I don't want to go to any restaurant or a coffee shop. The waiters keep staring.'

'Should we go to my apartment?' I asked

'We will be alone there. It won't look good, Atul.'

'Then we will ride like this for the next couple of hours.'

She kept quiet for some time and then said, 'Okay, let's go.'

I took utmost care to ensure that both of us entered the apartment separately. Once inside, we sat for some time on the mattress holding each other's hands. We talked about our respective futures; I told her about the interview I had just given.

'I am sure you will get selected,' she said assertively.

'How can you be so sure?' I asked.

'Because I know,' she held her pendant and began playing with it slowly.

We were alone in the apartment and were making excuses to touch each other gently. I moved close to her and spread my arms around her. I hugged her tightly and began kissing her passionately. Slowly, we lay down and my hand went under her kurta. I could feel the softness and roundness of her body. Her eyes were closed and her hands were tucked under my shirt. Excitement made our blood rush vehemently; we removed our clothes and held each other tightly. My arms surrounded her sleek waist and her arms encircled my shoulders.

I put a bedsheet on our naked bodies, and felt the softness of her body on me. For the next couple of minutes, we were tied together by the passion burning inside us, exploring each other. I tried to enter her. This was the first time for both of us and after several failed attempts, I finally succeeded. A cry of pleasure came from her; I felt the warmth of her body and kissed her gently. Both of us were taken in by this moment of fervour. After reaching the pinnacle of pleasure, we lay next to each other, breathing heavily. Those moments were eternal bliss.

It was getting late and Priya asked me to drop her at her office, and I obeyed reluctantly. After seeing her off, I came back to my room. The last five days had been a life changer. I had achieved what I had set out to. What began as confusion between love or lust, impressing the girl or falling for her, was over now. Priya was mine and I would never let her go away. That was the promise I made to myself that night.

I called up Priya late in the evening and we spoke to each other while lying on our respective beds. We both, admittedly, enjoyed the 'quality time' today and realized that a deep bond had been formed between us. It was magical. Once confused about my feelings for Priya, this relationship now seemed predestined to me. The sixth day was special. I had Priya by my side and was all set to be a corporate guy. Also, it was my birthday.

DAY 6

I woke up with my phone ringing near my head. It was my twenty-fourth birthday and my mother was calling me to wish me. The receiver was handed over to my father, who was uncomfortable wishing me. My father was not an expressive man and for him these little gestures meant overcoming a lot of inhibitions. His introverted nature was the primary reason I felt much closer to my mother.

Soon after I hung up, I was served a special chai by Lovely.

We relished each sip standing on the apartment's balcony overlooking the nearby garden, and shared anecdotes about Ramakant. Lovely left for work and I was waiting to hear from the human resources department of Wiretech. Meanwhile, I sent another leave application to Tectronics informing them of my prolonged sickness. Mr Bhanot may have had an idea about why I had fallen sick, but he never said it. Perhaps he was giving me time to leave, time to leave *gracefully*.

I was lost in these thoughts when my phone rang. It was Priya.

'Happy birthday!'

'Thank you.'

'Such a thanda response, Atulji.'

'If you were in front of me, I would have shown you who is thanda.' I teased.

'Shut up…don't you have anything else to do in the morning?'

I could imagine her making a face.

'What's the plan for the day?' I asked.

'Nothing, I will be in office and then I will take the evening Volvo back to Indore,' she replied.

'Can't you stay for a couple of more days?'

'I have already exhausted my "relative privilege points" by staying for a full week at Bhaiyya's house. Besides, I have to prepare the project report and do a timely submission. If I stay here any longer, you will not let me do so,' she replied mischievously.

'Can I drop you to the bus stand?' I asked.

'No, Rajesh Bhaiyya will drop me. We can only meet outside our office today.'

'See you in the evening then.'

We planted a goodbye kiss on our respective receivers and bade goodbye. I took a quick shower and then followed my family's instructions to go to a temple nearby to seek divine blessings. It felt odd to go to a temple a day after I had lost my virginity. But then I was thankful to God for the developments in my life, including my loss of virginity.

In my head, I had already planned a future with Priya, but was still working out some permutations and combinations. She was certain about a good placement and could easily get a job in any big city. I might have to move to Delhi if I received an appointment letter from Wiretech. Would she consider moving to Delhi?

As I closed my eyes to pray in the temple, I thought of calling Ahmed Ali. Ramakant had once told me that his students had a habit of calling Guruji on their birthdays as Guruji told them that there was a certain positive energy floating around on one's birthday and those blessings could take effect more easily. I never bought this logic, but decided to call Guruji anyway. He picked up the call and after exchanging pleasantries, he asked me, 'Are you happy?'

What is Ahmed Ali pointing at?

'I am happy, sir.'

'Good to hear that, Atul,' he replied. I wanted to tell him about Priya, yet for some reason I decided against it. 'Sir, please bless me on my birthday,' I requested.

'You will have to pay me gurudakshina for this,' said Ahmed Ali. Once again I did not understand him. I could sense he was smiling at this point. 'Atul, today is your birthday and it's an important day for you. Control your feelings and emotions, be your inner self today.'

With his blessings, he had left a code for me to decipher.

'Sir, what if I fail to do what you have asked of me?'

'Then my son, life has its own way of teaching you lessons,' he said in his calm voice.

I was confused. However, we said our goodbyes following which I went to my apartment. It was noon. Once again I was excited at the prospect of meeting Priya. She had an evening bus to catch. I wanted our meeting today to be the most memorable day of our lives. It was at this time that the doorbell rang and I opened the door. Charu was standing outside.

'Hey Charu, how are you? Welcome to my abode.' I tried to hide my astonishment.

She stepped inside carefully. Charu was wearing a skin-fit pink top and jeans, a very unusual choice of outfit for her. Her thin, small body was looking impressive in these clothes. I pulled a chair for her and dragged another stool so I could sit.

'So, Madam Charu. What brings you here?' She smiled and carefully took out a packet wrapped in shining paper from her bag.

'Happy birthday!' she said with a childlike smile.

'Oh, thank you. That's so nice of you,' I took the packet from her. She insisted I open it in front of her. It was a small Ganesh idol.

'Wow, this is really beautiful.'

Charu and I remained silent for a couple of seconds. She was looking around our messed-up apartment with immense curiosity.

'Have you taken leave from office?' I asked her.

'Yeah, I took sick leave,' she grinned.

'Let me get some tea for you,' I stood up.

'No, it's okay.'

'I will call Lovely also and check where he is. If he is not busy, maybe he can join us.' I was desperate to call for a cover for this encounter.

'No, don't call Lovely.' Charu held my hand and my pulse quickened.

'I don't enjoy his company, I enjoy yours,' she pulled herself dangerously close to me.

I tried to move away from her. 'Hey Charu, come on! What are you saying?'

'I mean it, Atul. Today is your birthday and I want to give you a present.'

'You have already given me one.' I had barely completed the sentence when she planted a kiss on my lips. I was dumbstruck for a moment and then pushed myself away from her.

'What are you doing, Charu? I cannot do this. Lovely is in love with you.' I was hoping this line would save me.

'But I am in love with you, Atul.' She hugged me and tried to reach out to my lips. Once again, I moved back.

'Charu are you in your senses?' I raised my voice.

'I am in my senses, Atul. I love you.' She held me again and kissed me. This time, I don't know why, I did not resist her. A certain passion aroused inside me and I responded back by holding her tightly. For that second I did not remember anyone, the sheer joy of experiencing another body overtook me. I surrendered to the darkness in me. At that moment, I remembered no one but Charu.

Deeply aroused, I lifted her and she crossed her legs around my body. I took her to a nearby table and stood in front of her, carefully observing each part of her body. Soon after, we found ourselves taking each other's T-shirts off. She was wearing a sports bra and the roundness of her body was sensual. We caressed each other. Her touch had been exciting, exciting enough for me to be completely lost in her.

The front door opened all of a sudden. My body as well as my mind froze. Lovely and Priya had come inside, carrying flowers and a birthday cake. I had forgotten to lock the door. Charu and I grabbed our T-shirts and tried looking at Priya and Lovely. Their faces reflected surprise, hatred and anguish. They had come to give me a pleasant surprise; I, in turn, had given them the shock of their lives.

Priya's eyes were blood red. She threw the flowers and cake on the floor and came close to me. As I tried to explain myself to her, my left cheek felt the warmth of her hand as she planted a tight slap on it. She turned away and went outside the apartment, crying. I did not have the courage to go after her. I knew I had lost Priya.

Charu quietly picked up her bag and moved out of the apartment. Lovely and I were alone now. I couldn't face Lovely, and against all odds tried to go near him. He pushed me aside with full force and I fell flat on the floor. He turned away and left the room.

I got up slowly and looked at the flowers lying on the floor. Each flower reminded me of the broken pieces of my life. I picked up the flowers one by one, and tried putting them together in vain. This was supposed to be the best birthday ever, but it had turned out to be my worst nightmare. I had ensured that it got ugly. I had lost my friend and a woman who I was in love with. These six evenings changed the course of my life.

Calling Priya turned out to be an exercise in futility. She did not take my calls, did not respond to my emails. She was gone. Rather, I had lost her. I shuddered each time I thought about what Priya must have been thinking about me. She had gone against her principles to be with me and I had failed her.

I went to the bus stop to catch a glimpse of her and apologize, but she was nowhere to be found. After waiting for two hours, I headed home. I could only imagine her travelling in the bus, sitting near a window, staring at nothing outside, her big black eyes filled with tears and anguish. Lovely had sent one of his friends to collect his stuff from his room; he had decided to stay with his friend and was not responding to my calls.

Sitting alone in the empty apartment, I cried aloud, hoping Lovely and Priya could hear me and come back. I wanted to go back and undo what had happened. There was no one else to be blamed. I had proved to be my own worst enemy.

A week later, I received an appointment letter from Wiretech and I resigned from Tectronics subsequently. Charu called me a couple of times but I did not take her calls. I wanted to run away from my past and seek refuge in a new city where I could make new memories. Delhi was a place that could accommodate my big dreams. It was an ocean of opportunities and I was ready to embrace it with open arms.

One day, Rajesh knocked on the door of my apartment. He was accompanied by three young lads. When I opened the door, he grabbed my neck, 'Bastard, I don't know what you have done with my sister. She left my home crying and Rakhi told me about your friendship with her. My impulse is to kill you but I have promised my sister I won't...' Before he could finish his sentence, the guy standing next to Rajesh packed a punch on my face. I have no memory of what happened thereafter.

Before I left Bhopal, I wanted to meet Saurav Bhanot, the man who had changed my fortune. We went to the same spot at the top of the hill. Sitting with him and smoking weed quietly, I remembered the advice Ahmed Ali had given me when I'd spoken to him. 'Be your inner self.' I had looked past my inner self and took comfort in the enchantment called lust. In other words, I had been a fool.

Once again, I made the mistake of not calling him and telling him about the course of events. Frankly, I did not have the nerve to speak to him. By now, the world of friendship and love that I had built for myself in Bhopal had crumbled. Perhaps to make way for the theatre of dreams that was New Delhi.

10

Delhi Beats

23 December 2012
DLF Phase-II Police Station
12.45 a.m.

MY BODY HAS become sore from sitting in one position for hours. I am lost in thoughts. The chill and the hard floor have numbed my bottom. My designer suit is no longer enough to provide warmth in this cold night. The cell smells of urine and blood. I feel like throwing up but then I look at the old man at the other end of the cell. He is fast asleep with his entire body covered in a blanket as if he is dead. I move and change my position, hoping against hope to catch some more warmth. I rest half my body against the wall and half against the cold iron rods.

I turn my head to look inside the police station. It is at its sleepy best. There are not many men around at this hour, just one hawaldar with a woollen cap and a thick sweater. I stare at the lone electric bulb, the only bright spark in an otherwise dingy room. This bulb is like me, lit alone in this night.

Shamsher Singh comes out of nowhere and asks me, '*Roti khai* (Did you eat)?'

'No, thanks.'

'*Re main tanne* five-star *ka* waiter *lage hoon ke?* Order *na le ra main, pooch raha hoon* (Do I look like a waiter in a five-star hotel. I am not taking your order, just asking you if you have eaten).'

Shamsher Singh reminds me of the ugly truth again.

'Thank you, sir. I am not hungry,' I say with a little more confidence this time.

'You are new. Slowly you will get used to it,' he smiles and moves away.

I cannot say anything to him. Surely, I will get used to it slowly. I cross my hands against my chest, hoping to keep my body warm. I lean my head against the wall and close my eyes. Once again, I go down memory lane. Memories, after all, will be my best companions in the coming days.

~

Eight years ago, I had wrapped up my life in Bhopal in two suitcases and had come to Delhi to chase my dreams. My new job, that of a field sales executive, kept me on my toes. I hung on to DTC buses and ate at numerous chhole kulche joints. Keeping up with the pace of the city proved difficult, but somewhere I was happy about fulfilling my parents' dream of working in an MNC.

Delhi is a city of contrasts. Once the political seat for every ruler who aspired to have political control over India to being a hotbed of modernity, the city has undergone a fascinating transformation. What I love about it is that every lane here represents these contrasts to perfection. Travelling through the ultra-hip Saket, you reach Mehrauli, which is home to the magnificent architectural wonder we know as Qutub Minar. And just when you think you are done, there is a Humayun's Tomb or a Red Fort standing with pride. Delhi lives in the present through its past. And so did I…eight years ago.

I rented a small one-bedroom apartment in the Paschim Vihar area. This time I was careful about not sharing it with any colleagues or friends. I had not completely healed from the heartbreaks in Bhopal and was thus afraid of new relationships. I wanted to be lonely alone rather than being lonely with someone else.

I was hired as part of Wiretech's aggressive marketing strategy, and as the newest entrant I was given a completely new set of customers who had never purchased anything from our company. These customers were called 'acquisition accounts'. An account, in sales parlance, means a clientele that had to be catered to. My brief was to get business from these customers. Most of my colleagues either pitied or scorned me when they took a good look at my customer list. One sales pundit even declared publicly, 'This *soorma Bhopali* will not be able to survive for more than six months because firstly, he has been a showroom sales person and secondly, he has no understanding of handling corporate clients.' They even began to mourn my predictable death as a failed salesman during their evening ritual of *sutte baazi*.

Initially, I struggled to even get an appointment, business was farther off. Every night, drenched in sweat and tired like hell, I came back to my apartment, washed myself with cold water, fed my hungry stomach with food packed in from a roadside dhaba and slept half-naked beneath an old fan. At times, I would tell myself, *Let's go back and leave the fucking place.* And the next moment, my resolve to stay in Delhi and slog my way to the top would grow stronger.

One fine day, Lady Luck decided to shine on me in the form of Finance Corporation Limited, one of those customers which buys from the same company again and again because it is never approached by any other company. Sales managers in our company thought they were a 'hardcore loyal' competition account. So nobody approached it, thinking it would not buy from Wiretech Insys.

It was no rocket science to figure out that since Finance Corporation Limited was regularly buying from our competitor, our competition had, therefore, not paid much attention to pricing. I demonstrated our products, which were technically better suited to its requirement. The committee was satisfied with my demonstration and all I had to do was to give them a price quote which was cheaper than the existing one.

Finance Corporation had a payment issue going on with its existing supplier and it was not exactly on great terms with them at that point of time. In short, it was a good time to turn it in our favour. By the end of our negotiations, Finance Corporation had agreed to give Wiretech Insys a supply order worth ₹75 lakh. On top of it, they reasoned that if our company could deliver and get the equipment installed in less time, they would do a 'rate contract' with us, which would ensure regular business for Wiretech Insys in the coming year. 'Rate contract' in business means that the quantity and price of the products to be purchased during a specific period of time are fixed between the buyer and seller. Finance Corporation was going for an expansion and hence there was a lot of business in store.

I had luckily stumbled upon this goldmine and planned to cash in on this opportunity to the fullest. I made a presentation to the higher ups in Wiretech Insys on the account 'acquisition' plan and drew a roadmap for business growth. Having impressed everyone, I was made the 'Account Manager' for Finance Corporation Limited. It was a more respectable term than a sales executive. An account manager is usually at the helm of affairs, managing and engaging external as well as internal resources ensuring continuous business from the customer.

~

Six months down the line, I was the official 'bright spark' of the company. We had ventured into the competition's arena, snatched its business and displayed exemplary leadership qualities. This also meant that I got a promotion after completing the probation period. It was now time for me to graduate to a motorbike. Many colleagues suggested that I should buy a second-hand bike, but my father, otherwise a man of few words, suggested, 'Son, a new vehicle is a new vehicle.' I got myself a new Hero Honda 'Splendor' and was very happy that day. I called up my childhood friend Golu to share the news of my new acquisition.

'*Jhakaas bade bhai,* you are our hero. Show these Dilliwalas what a true Chhattisgarhiya is,' he said. My colleagues who had predicted my 'grand failure' were eating their words. They rationalized my success by saying I had lucked out.

Luck, seriously? Ever heard of hard work, losers?

Be it luck or be it hard work, I enjoyed every bit of the success that I tasted. The speed at which I was riding my new bike had become a personal metaphor for my professional life as well.

Things kept on rolling like this. After I executed a couple of orders from Finance Corporation Limited, the General Manager (IT) referred me to a couple of his friends in the industry. Some of them were clean and some of them were, well, not so clean. The percentage of commission that got fixed with these 'not-so-clean' customers, varied between three to eight per cent, depending on the negotiating prowess of the customer and the size of the order. Being corrupt and encouraging corruption had now become my mantra to success. After every successful 'dirty' deal, I would remember James Bond telling his blonde girl after a night of fervour, '*What I did this evening was for the king and the country. It didn't give me any pleasure.*'

Selling my soul to the devil became a part of my job description. My flair for forming bonds with people instantly helped me crack one deal after another.

After spending two years in Wiretech Insys, I was branded the most promising, aggressive and confident young leader. Money kept coming to me thick and fast. I sold my bike and decided to get a new car for myself. After all, a leader does not ride a bike. My first car was an airconditioned Maruti Zen. When I drove it for the first time, I took it to the nearest temple. I faintly remembered the last time I had gone to a temple was on my twenty-fourth birthday. My life in Bhopal now seemed unreal. I had almost forgotten Lovely, Ramakant mailed once in six months, and I had not spoken to Ahmed Ali either, though at times I did think about what was happening to his Friends Club.

There was no news of Priya. I looked her up on all social networking sites, but there was no trace of her. I also checked upon her Raipur address with Golu's help. 'They moved out of the house a couple of months back and no neighbour has any idea where they are now,' Golu informed me over the phone.

I did find Rakhi on Facebook and messaged her, but she ignored me. I felt very bad; I felt as if they were treating me like a murderer. But then perhaps I was one; I had killed Priya's feelings. Yet I thought she should have given me at least one chance to speak, one chance to say sorry. By not allowing me to do that, she was being cruel.

My increasing wealth, my car and my bachelorhood ensured that I enjoyed female attention. My broken relationships had numbed me inside; I began to enjoy flirting with women and loved breaking their hearts. It gave me a sadistic thrill, and was also a defence mechanism against falling in love. Whenever I was with a woman, in my mind I was avenging what Priya had done to me.

My life went on a fast track and before I realized it, I had completed almost four years in Wiretech Insys. My 'aggressive' attitude and a 'go-getter' sales guy image took me to newer highs. I wielded enough power to get the management to fulfil my demands. I calculated a move, and asked to be transferred to a different team. It was the team that undertook large-enterprise-level projects countrywide. The members of this team had the highest visibility among the senior leadership outside India and they got all plum promotions.

The head of the team was Sushil Rajput. Designated a director, he was a short, clean-shaven, bespectacled man with a round face and a healthy and strong body. In his early 40s, Sushil was touted as one of the most powerful people in the company. Although he reported to the vice president, he had direct contact with the Singapore-based CEO of the company.

His team had fourteen members, who were equally divided between two team leaders. One of the team leaders was Veerendra Pratap Singh, a tall, clean-shaven man with a muscular frame. He wore thin glasses whenever he was low. He was an eternal Thakur and always boasted of his royal lineage from one of the little known kingdoms somewhere in eastern Uttar Pradesh. He had a remarkable sense of humour and was funny to the core. Many found his wit unmatchable. He was an ardent Amitabh Bachchan fan and wanted others to call him 'Amit' but everybody settled for Veeru instead.

He would often say, 'This chillar job is not for me, *yeh saala naukri* word is so demeaning. I want to own large farmlands where I can sit wearing long boots, a cowboy hat and sip beer in the afternoon.' I could never really figure out whether he was serious.

Veeru and I went on to become great friends. He was a genuine man with no air of superiority and he loved me the way I was. He was the first to congratulate me on the day I purchased my car. He came over to my apartment in the evening and we went for a test drive. As soon as we sat in the car, he pulled out a vodka bottle and asked me to stop at the nearest general store. We bought two bottles of cola, mixed it with the vodka and started our test drive in the lanes of Delhi. We often called this indulgence of ours, 'Car-O-Bar'. Most drivers in Delhi are known to be quite adept at this and play hide and seek with the traffic police.

The other team leader under Sushil Rajput was a witty Kashmiri lad, Anand Kaul. He was a handsome man and the brains behind all of Sushil Rajput's strategic deals and wins. He was an old timer in the market and had an extremely wonderful relationship with customers and various distributors and dealers of the company. Anand hailed from a rich Kashmiri family. He drove a posh SUV and had a collection of the most expensive wrist watches—from Tag Heuer to Tissot. Every part of his body flaunted a branded product. As fate would have it, I was made part of Anand Kaul's team.

'Welcome to the daredevil team, bachche. I have heard about you a lot—now is the time to excel. With a right mix of aggression and vision, you will be a champion,' Rajput told me when I met him formally for the first time. Calling his teammates bachche was part of his leadership skills. Incidentally, it was this gesture of calling me bachche that turned out to be an icebreaker between us; frankly, I was touched.

One of the biggest attributes of Rajput's team was its confidence in and respect for him. All of them swore by his name; they were like gladiators ready to die for him in the battlefield. Sushil, in turn, gave his team members complete freedom to bend the rules of the game they were playing. He protected his team members from anyone questioning their modus operandi. For him, victory counted the most. The end justified the means. As his newest recruit, I was dying to prove my mettle. Fortunately, I did not have to wait very long.

∾

A major oil company in Dehradun was going for a countrywide network implementation project. To win this deal, it was decided that Wiretech Insys would send one commander to the field post who would understand the customer's requirements and then 'influence' the way the project requirements were drafted.

The whole game was to position Wiretech's horse and the competition's elephant in the race so that the horse won the race easily.

The game was not as simple. So as a part of the strategy, the out location commander was to stay in Dehradun till the closure of the project, which was for a period of nearly six months. Since the work involved staying away from Delhi, no one in the team was keen to take up this project. I was the youngest recruit in the team without any family and hence this opportunity was presented to me.

My endeavour in Dehradun began with daily doses of dark rum in the evening with important 'decision makers' and 'influencers' at the oil company. As a part of the plan, I had to first develop a relationship with them, and then make them work for me.

My colleague Veeru, who was also in Dehradun for a project handover, came to meet me in my hotel. 'Philip Koda is coming tonight to our hotel. He is the deputy manager in the oil company and holds the key in the hierarchy,' I said. 'It's been almost two and a half months now. I have tried breaking into Philip's circle of confidence but this guy is a hard nut to crack. After great persuasion, I have managed to invite him today. We need to do something,' I told Veeru.

Veeru thought for a couple of seconds and said in his distinct UP accent, 'Bhaiyya, let's take him in our gear today.'

Philip Koda was a local pahadi and had a fair complexion, a thick brown moustache and a good build. He arrived at seven in the evening. He wanted to sit in the hotel room and drink as he wanted to avoid being 'seen' socializing with a prospective vendor of the oil company. Koda looked at Veeru with suspicion as he was not expecting him. I introduced Veeru to Koda and that brought some confidence in him. Once the ice was broken, Veeru engaged Koda in a conversation.

By the time we finished the bottle of rum, it was 10.45 p.m. Koda had enjoyed every bit of his time spent with Veeru and was mighty impressed by his understanding of 'trade' and the office politics involved in it.

'Kodaji, how many times have you gone to Mussoorie?'

'I have been there a number of times. I can't count,' replied Koda.

'I will take you to Mussoorie today through a special tracking route,' Veeru's eyes rounded themselves into Koda's eyes as if he was hypnotizing him.

'Really?' A drunken Koda accepted the challenge.

The three of us got up and headed towards our holy trail. I did not speak to Veeru and pretended to be equally drunk, thereby encouraging the 'cause'. I was wondering what this tall guy was up to.

We drove towards the other side of the city, and reached a lonely place. We slowly started our journey from the foothills, sipping rum and climbing up the mountain. The first half hour was smooth, but after some time the rum started taking its toll. We decided to eat something and then continue our journey. We gobbled the tandoori chicken we were carrying with us. After another half an hour of eating and some more sipping of the divine liquid, I felt like falling down and sleeping there itself. But this rest seemed to have charged Philip Koda; he stood up and was ready to move in the dense jungle in the dim moonlight.

We reached a stream and quenched our thirst with sweet mountain water. The way ahead was slippery. We walked by, stepping on small and big slippery stones for another ten minutes, and reached a narrow pass in the mountain, which had a steep fall on one side and slippery rocks on the other. 'Bhai logon, this is the most dangerous pass of the journey. I will go first and then hold your hands one by one to support you,' Veeru said.

Veeru passed the narrow passage first and said, 'Kodaji, your turn.' Koda looked at Veeru's hand, and walked five paces in the wet soil. I was relieved at the sight of Koda being in Veeru's safe hands, but the very moment I started walking, I saw Koda's hand slipping from Veeru's. Before I could catch him, he had fallen off from the narrow passage towards the steep side of the mountain.

'Kodaji!,' I shouted.

'Kodaji!' I shouted once again, my voice echoing back.

I looked up at Veeru's face; he was smiling. A deathly silence filled the atmosphere.

'Atul, Veeru, save me, yaar.' Koda's voice echoed in the darkness. Both of us looked at each other. Veeru moved his head in assurance and signalled me to take it easy.

'Kodaji, we are coming. Where are you?' Veeru shouted animatedly. He lit his mobile and I saw Koda's panic-stricken face at some distance. His body was fixed between two thick branches and he was holding one of the edges of the rock to support his upper body while his legs were floating in the air.

'Kodaji, hang on.' I also joined the club. Veeru got down on his stomach and I held his legs. He lowered his body and we carefully dragged our customer out of the mess. Koda was in a state of shock. Moments later, he hugged Veeru and me.

'You guys are my brothers. Had you not been there, I would

have been dead.'

If we had not been there, then you would not have been in that position either.

We shelved further plans of adventure and dropped Koda home.

'Explain yourself,' I asked Veeru.

'I have been to that place a number of times. There is no steep fall; in fact, there is a flat surface underneath the bushes and thick branches. We used to sit on those branches with our feet hanging. But at night, the view is deceptive and it comes across as if there is a steep fall but there is nothing below the branches.'

I shook my head in disbelief at Veeru's innovative way of breaking into the customer's 'circle of trust'. I took the cigarette from his hand and puffed.

It calmed me down, I wanted to crash.

With Koda on my side, I had access to key information that could help me win this deal. After six months of dedicated efforts, I returned to Delhi with a project worth ₹25 crore for the company, the biggest it had bagged in the past seven years.

When I entered the office, my colleagues applauded, whistled and patted me on my back. I wanted to float in this noise and never come out of it. Though there was noise in my surroundings, a silence was enveloping me. That day I missed listening to something in that noise.

11

Destiny Traversed

ANOTHER ONE-AND-A-HALF YEARS flew by, winning and losing big and small battles. I was now of one of the seniormost and trusted members of Sushil Rajput's core team and was swimming comfortably in the corporate ocean. At Wiretech, a financial year was divided into qualitative benchmarks. The point of setting these benchmarks was to keep the pressure and level of performance high while keeping the employees on their toes.

Our years were divided into halves of six months each, which were further sub-divided into quarters of three months and then month-ends. Every such qualitative mark in the year had some numbers and targets attached to it. I did not realize how time flew, chasing them one after the other. Almost all members of Sushil Rajput's team were promoted. My ascent was the fastest in the company. Anand Kaul and Veerendra Singh were also appraised and given decent pay hikes. Sushil himself had become the number two man in the company and was expecting to head it any time now since the managing director was on the verge of retirement.

Sushil had joined this company ten years ago as a sales manager; he had worked in a lot of small companies before that. With his amazing insight and leadership skills, he had risen to power in the company. Wiretech Insys had appointed distributors, who maintained ample stocks of the products from the company and sold these to dealers across the country. Distributors did not think twice before pumping any amount of money in the deal if Sushil was backing it. Sushil, in turn, returned the favour to these distributors by ensuring more-than-average profit margins to them by getting a good, discounted transfer price of the products from the company.

This was a deal-clinching combination. In business, the maximum revenue that a company makes by selling its products or services is called 'the top line' and the profit margin that the company makes by selling these products is called 'the bottom line'. The management of Wiretech Insys didn't mind selling products at discounted rates to the distributors as long as their top line and bottom line were met. The distributors didn't mind as long as their targets were met. The customers didn't mind as long as they were getting great MNC products and money as bribes on top of it for buying them. Sushil Rajput didn't mind getting promotions and pay hikes one after the other. And we didn't mind following a leader who had become the most influential person in the company.

I was earning more than enough now. I had bought a bigger car for myself and purchased a two-bedroom apartment in a posh locality in Noida. The house had all sorts of gadgets from a play station to a flat screen LED TV, to a home theatre and a mini bar. Now that I was well settled, my mother often called me to give me phone numbers of girls she had selected as candidates for my marriage.

I had most of the things that I needed in life at my disposal, yet there was a void. I had called Ramakant almost a year ago but had got a recorded voice message on his phone. He had replied to my email in which he had written that his consultancy business had earned good money for him and he was contemplating coming back to India and working with Guruji. I congratulated him and asked him to call me when he landed. Six months had passed but I had not heard from him. During lonely nights, ghosts of the past came back to haunt me. I thought about my life and friends in Bhopal. I had lost touch with almost all of them. I wanted to talk to Lovely again and find out what he was up to, but my ego did not allow me to do that. I often thought of Priya and wondered if we would ever meet again.

Sometimes, they say, lightning strikes at the right time. Sushil Rajput had just returned from a business trip to Shimla. He and Anand Kaul had gone to attend the executive briefing of the State Wide Area Networks (SWAAN) project. This briefing was conducted by the state government's IT secretary. All the leading IT and networking vendors across the country and the globe had been invited to the executive briefing of the project at the office of the central procurement agency of the state government.

SWAAN was an advanced telecommunication infrastructure, which was to be used extensively for exchange of data and other types of information between two or more locations, separated by significant geographical distances. Such wide area networks were to create a highway for electronic transfer of information in the form of voice, video and data that would work as a converged backbone network across different departments of the state. SWAAN was designed to cater to the information and communication requirements of all the state governments. The approximate evaluated value of this project was close to ₹100 crore.

My phone rang. It was Sushil Rajput.

'Yes, sir.'

'Meet me at Hotel Janpath at 8 p.m.,' Sushil never believed in explaining details over the phone.

'What's this?' Mitali asked.

'Nothing, SOS from the boss.'

'Something important?'

'Looks like.'

Mitali Bagga was the HR head. I was having coffee with her in the office cafeteria when my mobile phone rang. Mitali was a dangerously attractive woman. Born and brought up in Delhi, she had done her masters in human resource management from a reputed B-school in the capital. She was always dressed in crisp corporate suits and skirts. She was upfront and to-the-point in her talk, a suave woman who enjoyed her cigarettes as much as she relished her vodka. Mitali also had an imposing Spanish tattoo on her left ankle. Both of us got along quite well, and enjoyed each other's company.

I reached Hotel Janpath in Connaught Place in the evening. This majestic building and its imperial architecture takes you back in time the moment you enter its premises. After leaving the car in valet parking, I passed through the huge galleries of the hotel brilliantly lit by the most expensive of chandeliers. Corporate bigwigs dressed in crisp business suits went past me.

The TV- and AC-selling salesman had come a long way.

I entered the coffee shop and looked around for Sushil. I

saw him sitting with Anand Kaul along with one fat, short and bald guy in the corner.

'Hi, Atul,' Anand waved at me.

'Hi, good evening,' we shook hands.

'Let me introduce you guys. He is Mr Brij Kishore Chaurasia from Chaurasia Realtors. *Waise,* "realtors" is just the tip of the iceberg, sahib is into the stock market, energy, real estate, export, sports and what not.' Anand Kaul placed his hands on the fat guy's shoulders and gently pressed them to make him feel at ease. Chaurasia was obviously flattered. 'And he is Atul Shukla, the quintessential stud. He is one of the most dynamic and energetic young growing leaders in our company.' Praising me to high heavens was part of Anand Kaul's plan to position me in the right context with Chaurasia as I was the one who was going to front-end the new battle.

Sushil Rajput now intervened. 'Atul is part of my core team—feel free to discuss anything with him. He is like my own kid.' Chaurasia's red eyes, which were bulging out of his round, chubby face stared at me and I could not do much except to smile back at him.

'Chaurasiaji came with us from Shimla after attending the executive briefing for the SWAAN project, and he will be our chief ally and mentor in this case,' Rajput told me. I looked at Chaurasia from the corner of my eye; he was sipping the expensive coffee. 'Chaurasiaji has an extremely cordial relationship with the IT minister in the state. He has assured us that if we promise to take good care of him, he will ensure that we will be the beneficiary of the project. He will help get our payment back in time and help us in the successful execution of the project with complete support from the government's red tape,' completed Sushil Rajput.

This supposedly lesser known business tycoon is the middleman of the IT minister of the state?

'What's the catch?' I placed the coffee cup back on the table after taking a few sips.

Anand Kaul was ready for this question. 'Atul, the IT secretary of the state is a mere pawn in the hands of the IT minister. He will do whatever the minister asks him to do. He does not know the ABC of IT. In his last role, he was the IT secretary for the department of agriculture. As a matter of fact, his posting has been strategically positioned by the minister to make sure that he does not create any obstacles in the minister's plan to roll out different IT initiatives in the state. It's a win-win strategy by the minister—he can position himself as one of the most modern, forward-looking IT ministers in the state, while his personal wealth keeps on multiplying.'

'If Chaurasiaji has good relations with the minister and the IT secretary is of no relevance and the game is so smooth, then where are we stuck?' I inquired

Sushil Rajput intervened. 'D&Y, the global leader in consultancy, has been appointed as the consultant by the government for this project. It has been appointed after getting a cabinet-level sanction. Once the Request for Information (RFI) document containing the scope of the project has been released and the executive briefing is conducted between the vendors and the government, the vendors will be submitting their respective technical proposals for the project. D&Y will evaluate these proposals and rate them in the order of 1, 2 and 3. These rankings will be given on the basis of technical compliance and competence of the solution, and then these three selected vendors will be given the opportunity to bid in the tender. The successful bidder will be finalized from among them.'

'This means we need to feature in the first three rankings,' I asked.

'Absolutely,' Anand Kaul took over from Sushil Rajput this time. 'Once the offer to submit the commercial bid is made to us, Chaurasiaji will ensure that we win the bid.' Anand looked at Chaurasiaji for another round of assurance.

'Is there any problem getting in the first three ranks?' I was getting to the bottleneck. There was a long pause. Sushil looked at Anand and told me, 'There are two issues in the qualification criteria. One is certification and the other is prior experience.' I looked at Chaurasia; he was listening to us. We were discussing our shortcomings outside our inner circle before the battle. It was a dangerous thing to do. Sushil understood my concerns. He gently closed his eyes and shook his head to assure me that it was all-right.

'One of the certifications required is for the "Restriction of the Use of Hazardous Substances in Electrical and Electronic Equipment (RoHS)", which the qualifying products should have. These are European standards and almost every company nowadays in this business has them, except us. We have requested our corporate head office and the R&D team in Singapore to get these done as soon as possible but our team there believes that these certifications are more of an engineering issue rather than a commercial one.'

'And what's the second issue?' I asked candidly. 'According to the second qualification criteria, "the bidder should have prior experience of executing such projects in India and globally", and we are falling short there too,' said Anand.

'This is a big system integration project. Why can't we bid as a consortium with other players in a similar field who qualify in accordance with the evaluation criteria?' I asked. Consortium is a term used when two or more companies shake hands on participating in a single big project.

You scratch my back and I will scratch yours.

'That would have been much easier,' Sushil interjected, 'but Wireless Insys has acquired Zentech, one of the leading system integrators in the world, and our global management wants us to bid for this project as a full-fledged system integrator. The global experience is met by Zentech's past execution of such projects but for the Indian experience, we will outsource it to GenNext Corporation.'

'GenNext, the Indian company we had outsourced parts of many of our other projects to? But why GenNext? They are okay, but too small a company for us to partner with for such a big project.' I looked at Sushil.

'GenNext is one of the companies owned by Chaurasiaji,' Sushil answered my question. The picture was now beginning to get clearer. Chaurasia was a close ally of the IT minister. He would help Wiretech Insys get the big project. Wiretech Insys would, in turn, give business to his company by outsourcing a part of the project to it. This was a nice way of paying for Chaurasia's effort without getting caught by the tax authorities.

'Don't be surprised, Atul. What you are witnessing today is nothing new, this arrangement of having a small company as a partner by a bigger company is an existing measure of the corporate underbelly. It makes things that much easier and smoother,' Sushil rationalized.

'This means the entire game plan is set. We bid for the

project with relative newcomers in the game, get evaluated and recommended by the consultants despite our shortcomings. Chaurasia*ji* then pitches in and helps us win the project with our hiked prices. We outsource part of the project to one of his companies and the entire mammoth project is executed smoothly across the state, the payments collected in the shortest of time, kickbacks paid in time and we add another feather in our profitability and establish ourselves as leading system integrators in the country,' I summed it up.

'Perfect,' Sushil said.

'And the bottleneck of the entire project remains with the consultants,' Anand Kaul explained, 'They hold the key to our recommendation.'

'And that's where you come in the picture,' Sushil continued. 'When I was in Shimla last week for the executive briefing for the project, the consultant's team was there too. Believe me, they are bunch of real good-looking, smart women and I am sure my James Bond will be able to influence them.'

Eh, he wants me to be a sex toy, screw the ladies and get the recommendation?

'But if the IT minister is on our side, why can't we use him to influence the consultants to ease the evaluation criteria?' I asked.

'The consultants are selected by an independent cabinet committee at the centre in consultation with the Ministry of Law, and we don't have any influence over them,' Chaurasia said.

'We'. Interesting!

'Then why would the minister play such a risky game? There is a possibility that "we" might not make it to the final three.' My question did not go down well with Sushil. He opened his mouth to answer me but was cut short by Chaurasia. 'Mr Atul, this is not about the minister. He has released a bounty and if it's not you or I, some other hunter will join the feast,' Chaurasia smiled when he said the last sentence.

'Besides, Atul, this is a ₹100-crore project, the biggest ever to be executed by Wiretech Insys in the history of its business. If we get this, I move to the position of MD, Anand Kaul takes on my position and you are promoted as a country manager for sales in this vertical. Being a country manager in such a short time is a feat not many have achieved.'

We shook hands for the last time in the evening and left. My role in the biggest play of my life had been charted out. I had to get the consultant to recommend our company regardless of its shortcomings. I drove back to my home in NOIDA. I had a little less than a week to study the documents, prepare the plan and come up with justifications as to how I would tackle the evaluation criteria hurdles and then had to get them accepted by the consultants before the due date of submission.

All in a span of six days and six evenings.

12

The Game Begins...Again

Wiretech Insys's corporate head office is located in DLF cyber city, Gurgaon. DLF, which has become synonymous with Gurgaon, has the lion's share of real estate developed around this satellite city. Gurgaon's development in the last decade has taken many by surprise and most are awed by it. A famous English writer once said, 'The amount of infrastructure development that has happened in Gurgaon in the last five years had not been done in the UK for the last fifteen years.' Be it soaring skyscrapers, ever-widening roads, construction of the metro, frequent traffic jams or the late night life of the 'government-approved' drinking places mushrooming in every nook and cranny, the city has something to offer to everyone.

I was sitting in my cubicle the next day in our corporate head office. The request for information (RFI) document had all the functional requirements of the project and I had to 'map' Wiretech Insys products, services and solutions in accordance with the project's requirements. This was a huge project and no stone could be left unturned.

'Hi, Tiger, busy?' Veerendra Singh came to my cubicle.

'Hi, Veeru. I need to study these documents to prepare a response. There is a lot of technical mumbo jumbo in them.'

'Which one is this?' Veerendra looked at the RFI document. 'SWAAN,' I replied

Veerendra eyes twinkled. Was he surprised because the big bosses had chosen me over him? Or did he have an intuition about the project? 'SWAAN. This is interesting,' he flipped through a couple of pages and looked at me. I was still deep into the papers; he walked a couple of paces and then turned towards me and said, 'Atul, this is big, much more than you can ever imagine. Be careful. Don't think I am scaring you, but it's my word of advice. You can reach me whenever you feel like doing so.'

I got up from my cubicle and walked up to him to clasp his shoulders. 'I know you will always be there for me.'

Veerendra smiled back at me and went to his cubicle. I came back to my seat and immersed myself in the deep pile of papers. I had two triumph cards in terms of justifications. One was the system integration arm of Wiretech Insys, which was recently acquired and had executed similar projects outside the country; hence the condition of having an Indian experience should be relaxed. And the other was to propose the equivalent certification with US standards on the same lines as the European standard that was asked for. Although the tests conducted in these two certifications were different, they proved to be more or less the same. There were in total five certifications asked for and we were complying with all except two.

I was not going to place my triumph cards on the table immediately; I looked at the two business cards handed over to me by Anand Kaul: Suhana Gupta and Ritesh Agarwal. Their designations read 'Senior Director'.

Consulting firms often give such heavy designations to their people.

I fixed up an appointment in the evening. The D&Y group's office was right next to ours. I decided to walk up to them. Before leaving the office for the meeting, I went up to Anand Kaul's cabin and discussed my day's effort. We mutually agreed on the strategy of listening first and delivering later.

Dressed in a crisp, expensive business suit, I got down from my building on the road and walked towards the D&Y office. It was mid-December and winter was at its peak. I reached the D&Y office and waited at the reception for Suhana Gupta and Ritesh Agarwal. The office boy asked me to sit inside the cabin that had a nameplate 'Vichaar' affixed to the door.

After five minutes, the door opened and in came Suhana along with Ritesh. Suhana was a short and thin lady in her late 20s. Her fair complexion and oval face was a little less than attractive. She wore a tight shirt and pants, which seemed to be a desperate attempt at accentuating her assets. Ritesh Agarwal, on the other hand, was your metrosexual 'dude'—perfectly gelled hair, broad shoulders, bespectacled in Versace frames. He was perfect photo shoot material for any business magazine.

Neither of them looks senior. Let's see what pearls of wisdom they have to offer.

'Hi guys, I am handling the SWAAN project for Wiretech Insys,' I introduced myself, exchanging plastic smiles.

'What would you like to have? Tea? Coffee?' Ritesh asked.

'A tea would do,' I replied. Ritesh looked at Suhana who settled for a coffee.

'My office is right across the road. I just walked across to your office. Was lucky to get some exercise today,' I placed my hands on my newly formed little paunch. Suhana smiled; so did Ritesh.

'Do you guys get time to exercise?' I continued with my good health mission. 'Ritesh, I am sure you do spend quite some time exercising, don't you?' It was time to flatter Ritesh now. 'Oh not really, just a couple of tennis games on the weekends. That's it,' he replied.

'That's really great. You know, the kind of life we lead these days, it's really great that you can spare some time for your body. It is good for the overall work-life balance.' In the meantime, tea and coffee were being served on the table in front of us. Ritesh gestured for all of us to start enjoying the hot beverages.

'And you, Suhana?' I tried to probe into her regimen.

'Me? No way. I am a complete foodie and don't exercise at all.'

'Doesn't look it, though,' I smiled and sipped the tea. Her smile indicated that she was suitably flattered.

From weather conditions to traffic problems, we covered a range of topics in a short span of time and now I wanted to talk business. 'By the way, on this current SWAAN project, what is your take on the qualification criteria?' I made this sound extremely inconsequential.

'Those are global standards, that's it,' Ritesh replied.

'But why only a couple of those specific standards?' I stressed.

'Are there any issues with you guys in those standards?' he probed.

'Not exactly, but yes I would like to have a debate or a discussion on those standards. I can give you my justifications as to why a couple of them are not relevant and can be met by alternate standards.'

Now that all three of us were on one page, I decided to play my cards. I told them where we stood on the qualification criteria and how the Indian experience should be relaxed since we had just acquired a global company that had done similar projects elsewhere in the world. I explained to them that Wiretech Insys's stand on the environmental certifications that we intended to comply with for the project were not relevant in the Indian context. Both of them gave me a patient hearing for almost forty-five minutes.

'Atul, you have a relevant point. You need to put it across in an email and send it to us. We will think over it.'

The game was half won; I was beginning to get up when Ritesh said, 'Atul, why don't you wait for a minute? Since this is an important issue, I will call my team leader also and have her views on the table too.'

I nodded my head in affirmation.

Ritesh went out and I chatted up Suhana in his absence. I was anyway going to need her help to turn the decision in our favour. Ritesh came back in ten minutes, followed by a girl with straight hair dressed in light grey trousers and a black full-sleeved shirt. She was looking at some documents when I turned my head to look at her.

It's her!

She looked at me, her eyes expressing the shock and

bewilderment she must have felt seeing me after eight long years. Priya Arya looked as beautiful now as she did back then. The chubbiness of her cheeks had given way to a more toned look. Her once innocent demeanour was now more probing, demanding nothing but professionalism. Ritesh introduced her as the associate vice president of D&Y. We shook hands quietly. I was still benumbed by this twist of fate, though she was calmer and more composed.

We sat around the table and Ritesh and Suhana briefed Priya about the entire discussion we had had earlier. I didn't know whether she was listening and paying attention to what her colleagues were explaining to her. I could not hear what was being said. I wanted the world to come to a standstill so that I could hold Priya in my arms and apologize. I imagined myself as Rishi Kapoor in white from the film *Sagar* singing '*Waqt ka dariya behte behte is manzar mein tham jaaye*...(May the river of time stop in this moment).'

'Atul! Atul,' Ritesh shook me out of my reverie.

'Yeah...yes?' I looked at him.

'We need to sit on this issue and then come back to you. Meanwhile, as discussed, you send us an email with detailed explanations and justifications,' said Suhana.

'Sure,' I looked at Priya. I was hoping she would say something, but she did not. I got up to leave and shook hands with Ritesh and Suhana. The moment I extended my hand to Priya, she took her BlackBerry and began punching in a number. She excused herself and moved out of the room. I followed her, but she walked past the reception area and moved inside the office, using her digital ID badge.

She does not want to speak to me.

I walked towards my office. Priya was cold towards me and understandably so. I had tried spotting any signs of matrimony on her body—mangalsutra, sindoor, bangles—but there was nothing.

But then she had always been a career woman.

The fact that I chanced upon Priya again at the same time when I had to work on the most important project of my life was no coincidence. It had already happened once. Only this time, the two things were intertwined. Being an AVP, Priya must be in a position to influence the team to get the required changes in the qualification criteria. But would she do it? The prospect of mending a broken heart and getting the deal for my company seemed daunting. But I had already planned a 'Project Priya' in my head. I would beg for forgiveness, explain the importance of the project, ask for her help and then ask for her hand in marriage and never let her walk out of my life. How blissful would life be!

DAY 2

I drafted the email carefully and went to Sushil Rajput's cabin to discuss it with him. Sushil read the mail and suggested some language changes here and there. Being the king of diplomacy, he knew exactly how to make a letter effective. He handed over the printout to me and said, 'How confident are you of getting this representation accepted and getting through?'

'We need not worry, sir. I know the AVP. Priya Arya is a good friend of mine and I have known her since her college days.' I emphasized the words 'good friend'.

Sushil flashed a smile when he heard this. 'That's like my stud,' he got up and patted my back. I felt like a stallion in the stable of Sushil Rajput, neighing, jumping and puffing air through my nose, ready to mate with the next mare.

I reached my desk and called up Suhana Gupta. I wanted to take Priya's email ID and phone number. A strong sense of déjà vu came over me; it reminded me of how I had called Rakhi eight years ago on her mobile.

'Hi, Suhana, this is Atul from Wiretech Insys.'

'Hi, Atul.'

'How are you doing?'

'I am good. What about you?'

'Good. So I was about to send you and your team the email that we discussed last evening. I wanted to check if it will be okay if I mark a copy of this mail to Miss Priya Arya.' I was careful to add the word Miss.

'Yes. It is priya.arya@dny.com.'

'Great, Suhana,' I paused for some seconds and then said, 'Can you share Miss Arya's phone number with me?' Priya was not some senior government bureaucrat who wouldn't share her phone number with a lesser mortal like me. After a pause that lasted a few seconds, Suhana said, 'I really don't know, Atul. You can ask her yourself if you want to.'

'That's perfectly okay, Suhana. I was wondering just in case our MD wants to meet you guys, I would be required to fix up an appointment for him. If there is someone assisting her, you can give me his or her number or else I might call you and trouble you to arrange a meeting.' I had played my cards just right. I was comparing Suhana to Priya's assistant, which she was not and just to prove a point about her seniority, she gave me Priya's number. It was not a Delhi number.

'This doesn't look like a North India number. Where is

Miss Arya based?' I asked Suhana.

'She is based in Bangalore and has come here for a week to oversee the evaluation work with us,' she replied. I thanked her and cut the line. I looked at the number and decided to call her. My heart was pounding as I dialled her number. After a couple of rings, the line got connected.

'Hello.' It was Priya's voice.

'Hi, Priya, this is Atul.'

'Atul, I am in a meeting. I can't talk right now.'

'I am sorry, Priya, I really am. After that evening in Bhopal, I tried to search for you everywhere but I could not find you. I could not speak to Rajesh about you, Rakhi didn't respond to my calls. You didn't even give me a chance to present my side of the story. I know no amount of reasoning can justify what I did but at least meet me once and give me a chance to speak.'

'I don't want to talk to you on that subject any more. I will appreciate it if you don't call me again,' she hit me point blank.

Accepting rejection was not my cup of tea. 'If that is the case, Miss Arya, then if not personally, I would like to meet you professionally and you cannot deny me that right. I have sent you and your team a mail and I need a reply on that.'

'We will look into it and get back to you,' she said and cut the line.

I slammed my hand hard on the desk.

Damn! What have I done!

I wanted to say sorry and win Priya's trust. But my ego had come in the way. Fate had put me in the race once again to get Priya in these six evenings and I had ruined it by being curt. I felt like destiny's pampered child who was given a chance to correct his wrongs but who had messed it all up again. With only five days left, I did not have much time on my hands. It was 4 p.m. when I decided I should meet her. The D&Y office might not have been a good idea considering Priya could be accompanied by her colleagues. And so I decided to meet her at the hotel where she was staying. If only I knew the name of the hotel.

After about an hour, I called the D&Y reception and asked them to connect me with Priya. 'I am Viraat calling from Radisson Hotel, Gurgaon. We have a room reservation for Miss Priya Arya from the D&Y group. I wanted to confirm the booking for her.'

The receptionist forwarded the call to Priya.

'Yes.'

'Good evening, ma'am. I wanted to confirm your booking with us.'

What a method actor I am!

'Listen, I haven't made any booking in your hotel.'

'Oh really, but our relationship team informed me about the room booking with us.'

'No. You need to cancel it if there is any such reservation at all.'

'No issues, ma'am. We will cancel the booking,' I held the line and made noises on the keyboard for an authentic feel. 'Thank you for holding the line, ma'am. As a part of the customer relationship programme, can I take a minute of your time to get some feedback?'

'Yes,' she said slowly.

'Since the D&Y group is one of our premier customers and most of your colleagues stay with us, may I know the specific reason for your not choosing us to stay with us, ma'am?'

'It is the proximity to my office.'

'Thank you, ma'am. Just a last question, where are you staying, ma'am?'

There was a pause for a second. 'That should not concern you,' she said.

Oops, I am losing the plot!

'That's perfectly all right, ma'am. But if you could please help me complete the form, it will be very kind of you,' I sounded like a desperate intern.

My continuous use of 'ma'am' and kindness had had an effect on Priya.

I know her so well.

'I am staying at the Crowne Plaza, Gurgaon,' she cut the line.

Gotcha!

I wiped the sweat beads from my temple and reached Crowne Plaza at 6 p.m. I would wait till Priya got back, hopefully alone. The grand entrance to Crowne Plaza, Gurgaon, is as elegant as it is opulent. The freshness of the ambience and the coolness of the atmosphere inside the lobby caught my fancy. Huge chandeliers were shimmering as I walked on the shining marble floor. I checked for Priya Arya and I was informed that she had still not reached the hotel. I sat in the lobby with my gaze fixed towards the entrance.

As I was waiting for Priya in the grand lobby, I remembered waiting for her sitting on the bike in the parking of her office eight years ago; a beautiful girl dressed in a simple salwar kameez would come out in the evening. A little shy, a little confident, she would walk straight towards me. Years later, she was a hardcore corporate woman, but as beautiful and charming as ever.

At around 7.30 p.m., I saw Priya stepping out of a car and

waving goodbye to someone. I could not see who it was and I was consumed by jealousy. But I could not lose my grip now, I reminded myself. She saw me as I got up from my seat. She did not seem particularly surprised.

Was she expecting me?

I wanted to leave no stone unturned to impress her. So I had worn an expensive Van Heusen business suit and kept a Mont Blanc pen in my breast pocket. I wanted to convey the idea that I was doing well in life. Priya walked straight towards me, and I smiled, 'Hello, Priya.'

'Why have you come here?' she said.

'Listen Priya, I want to talk to you for ten minutes. After that, I will accept whatever you say. But please give me at least one chance.'

After an initial hesitation, she agreed. 'There is a famous Brazilian restaurant here. I am hungry, let's go there.' We both walked towards the restaurant. It seemed like a long walk towards our table. There was awkwardness between us. I ordered one cabidela, rice and beans.

'How did you come to know I am staying here?' she asked.

'Ah that's not important,' I stopped her round of inquiries. 'Priya, I know you felt cheated when you saw me and Charu together and no one except me is to be blamed for this. That day Charu came and expressed her feelings for me. I tried to stop her, but I couldn't. It was not only about you, it was about Lovely as well. In one day, I lost both of you, and a part of me died that day. Lovely liked Charu and in one second, my old friendship with him was finished. You left me too and I was destroyed. It's not a justification but at that age I always found myself struggling between love and lust, gratification and commitment. Maybe I was not ready for the responsibility of a relationship then. All these years, I have tried to gather all that can make me happy but I have never been fulfilled. I have remained unhappy from the inside; I have felt a void deep inside and I cannot live with it any longer. I am sorry for what I did to you, please forgive me.' I was almost in tears.

There was nothing but silence between us. She was looking straight into my eyes.

'Atul, you need not be apologetic. I am no one to forgive you. You said a part of you died that day, but I say I died that day. You did not just break a relationship, you broke my trust. My trust, Lovely's trust. You said you live in a void—I say ever since that day I have become a void. You don't know how it feels to grow up as a girl who has lost her father and has a young sister to look after. The whole world tends to take advantage of you at every stage. I felt hurt because I trusted someone who did exactly that.' Her red eyes revealed more than her words.

I placed my hand gently on Priya's hand, and she was taken aback. 'Priya, God has given us one more chance to fix things. We can't move on if we keep discussing what happened eight years ago. The fact is I still love you and will always love you. Can we keep everything aside and start afresh? I can't live without you, Priya. I need you,' I came close to begging.

'This is not possible, Atul. I am seeing someone.'

These words hit me like a speeding rock from space. I paused for a moment and then gathered myself.

'That's not a problem. Since I was not around, it was natural for you to start seeing someone. But now that I am back, we should see each other.'

Priya was taken aback at the ease with which I expressed

my desire. 'Listen, Atul, it is not as simple as you think. I just can't press a delete button and finish off everything in my life and begin afresh with you. I can't do the same to anyone else. Maybe God made us meet so we could settle old scores. And why should I believe you? You have ditched me once, you can do it again.'

That question was intended to show the mirror to me. Before I could reply to it, the waiter came with our food. We paused for a moment and let the waiter do his job. Then we ate quietly. Priya's assumption that I may ditch her again was bothering me. I didn't have an answer to that. Was I so desperate because I wanted Priya back? Or was it because she was the decision maker in one of my challenging assignments?

When the waiter took away our empty plates, I tried to reason with her again. 'You have to believe me, Priya. You want me to jump off from Signature Towers to prove myself? I can do that...'

She did not look impressed and cut me off mid-sentence. 'Atul, you said ten minutes. I think those are long over. I need to go, I have a busy schedule ahead. As far as your official mail on the SWAAN project is concerned, all I can say is that we can't do anything on the guidelines. They have been approved by our team of experts and a panel of government officials. We can't just change that overnight. You will receive an official communication tomorrow from us.' She stood up and started moving.

'Priya, is this personal?'

'No, Atul. It's business.'

DAY 3

Sleep evaded me. I kept sending 'I love you', 'I miss you' text messages to Priya after every one hour. For me, winning her back took precedence over getting the tender conditions tweaked in Wiretech Insys's favour. If at all, this would be the second stage. I had to be close enough to Priya first.

I reached office at around 11 a.m. I looked sleep-deprived, and Veerendra Singh was quick to point that out. 'Hey Tiger, what's keeping you up at night? You look fucked.' I smiled back at him. 'Come, let's have a coffee.' He placed his hand on my shoulders and we walked towards the office cafeteria.

The office cafeteria was swarming with people having breakfast. To be able to eat in the morning at home was considered a luxury as the office started early. We searched for an isolated corner and sat there with cups of coffee in front of us.

'Is this the new project, SWAAN, you are busy with?' he asked.

'Yes, it is.'

'Very short reply. Tell me if I can help you in any way.' Veerendra was always the first one to offer help to me when I was in need. I remembered his 'help' in Dehradun when we 'trapped' Kodaji and he became our guiding light for the rest of the project.

I trusted Veeru so I told him the entire story.

'You mean to say you cheated on that girl and lost her. And now when she is back in your life, you want to cheat her again by asking her for a favour because that is the most important thing for you in life. *Wah, kya* love story *hai*, Mr Atul Shukla! Either you get your priorities right or keep hanging purposelessly forever,' he said bluntly.

'But why do you think I am asking for a "favour" per se? If she loves me, she will obviously understand me. My gain is her gain, so where's the problem?' I tried to reason.

'Don't be a kid, Atul. There is something called work ethics. You cannot expect a person to be ethically wrong just because he or she loves you. And by the way, why would she even do it for you? What have you done for her? You were caught naked with another girl just a day after you slept with her.'

'I was half-naked,' I clarified. 'I have not come here to be preached at, you know. She would do it for me because I love her and she loves me too.'

'Great! I guess you and Sourav Ganguly draw confidence and keep playing on despite poor form.' Veeru sipped his coffee.

'Nice joke, look, I am dying laughing... Listen Veeru, I am stuck. I don't know what to do. I have already committed this deal to Sushil, and he has already made plans with Anand Kaul and Brij Kishore Chaurasia of GenNext.' Veeru looked at me sharply when I mentioned the name Brij Kishore Chaurasia.

'Chaurasia? Have you met that fatass?'

'Yes, we met over coffee a few days back.' I told him about my meeting with Sushil, Anand and Chaurasia, but carefully chose to omit the parts where I was promised a promotion.

'If Chaurasia is involved, you cannot back out from this deal, Tiger,' said Veerendra.

'I didn't get you.'

'I am going to tell you something but you have to keep it to yourself. Promise me you will not discuss this with anyone.' Veeru looked straight into my eyes; I nodded in agreement.

'Sushil Rajput is a silent partner in GenNext along with Chaurasia. He has put his money in the firm, and all the big deals are either billed through GenNext or are outsourced to it. So Sushil makes money every time GenNext gets business, the same business which he controls anyway.'

I was shocked. Sushil was using his position to influence the business that Wiretech Insys was outsourcing to GenNext, and since he was one of the partners in GenNext, he was earning money from both sides.

How dirty can this corporate world be?

'How come none of the compliance officers and other senior officials of the company know about this?' I asked.

'All I can say is Sushil alone cannot live with the entire booty. If he has to survive and thrive in this system he has to keep all those concerned happy, which he does by sharing the booty with all the right people.'

'You mean to say the MD is aware of this partnership and he is also one of the beneficiaries of this arrangement?'

'He could be.'

'But how do you know all this?'

'Tiger, I have worked long enough with Sushil to get under the skin of his arrangement. Don't be so surprised—this is just one of the dark aspects of the underbelly of the corporate world. There are arrangements between the marketing department and the ad agencies of companies. People take their "cut" for influencing the business that a dealer gets from the company. These things happen. This is part and parcel of life. At the end of the day, we are all human beings. If there are good ones, there are bad ones too.' Veeru had exposed me to one of the most damning truths of life with ruthless ease.

I sat quietly for a while, still processing the information. I had always respected and admired Sushil Rajput for all that he had achieved in life. But I had just been exposed to one more side of Sushil Rajput's business acumen. He was riding high on the success of others; suddenly the respect and admiration that I had for him gave way to jealousy and a sense of being cheated. I didn't know how to react: Should I stop him? Should I go and fight with him? Should I close my eyes and ears and let things go the way they are or should I take a cue out of his book and do something similar for myself?

'I know what you are thinking, Tiger, I felt exactly like same way but I dared not be a whistleblower. I don't have the balls to be one. And my conscience does not allow me to get into any kind of hanky-panky to make money for myself. Hence I have sorted out a middle path for myself, the one Gandhiji taught us, *bura mat dekho, bura mat suno, bura mat bolo* (don't see bad, don't hear bad, don't speak bad). I do my work and don't worry about them, Gandhiji didn't tell us *bure ko roko* (stop the bad),' Veeru replied.

I felt amused, and at once understood the meaning of 'power tends to corrupt and absolute power corrupts absolutely'.

'Is Anand Kaul also party to it?' I asked.

'There's a high probability,' replied Veerendra. I was irritated by Veeru's attitude. Why was he not sure of anything? Maybe he was left alone in the syndicate and was trying to spill the beans as a way of getting back at the people in it.

'Veeru, I am now neck-deep in this shit. What should I do? I need your help.'

'You are destiny's special child, Tiger, and I am jealous of that. It's your battle and no one else can fight it for you. On the one hand, you have a career and on the other, you have love. It's not what abilities we have in us but what choices we make in life that make us who we are.'

Veeru's words left me speechless. I turned around and looked outside the building. People dressed in crisp suits and elegant ties were walking hurriedly from one place to the other. They were chasing a dream. Like me they, too, must have prayed for success. But what does 'success' mean? Is their idea of success different from mine? Are ethics important when you are running after your dream?

My thoughts were cut short by a buzz. I looked at my phone and saw a mail from Suhana of the D&Y group. I looked across at Veeru who was busy on the phone with one of his clients. I did not want to disturb him, so I waved goodbye and hurried towards my desk.

I opened the mail and my heart stopped beating. It was a polite and diplomatic refusal to make changes in the qualification criteria. My justifications were point-by-point counter-justified and turned down. I wasn't sure if this was Priya's way of getting even with me or if she was just being a thorough professional.

I could not afford to take 'no' for an answer and decided to meet them. Personal meetings have an edge over phone calls or written letters. I wanted to check the body language of Suhana, Ritesh and their team. It was important for me to understand the purpose behind the refusal so that I could plan my next move. I walked across to the D&Y office and asked the receptionist to call for Suhana. After waiting for five minutes, she turned up.

'Hi, Suhana, I am sorry I didn't call first.' I walked up to her and shook her hand.

'No issues, tell me,' she moved her head swiftly.

'I read your mail and since I was coming back from a meeting I thought of having a word with you guys.'

Suhana looked uneasy and she did not make any effort to conceal it. 'I have not booked any meeting room. Come inside my cabin and we will have a chat there.' She asked the reception to make an entry for me and I took the visitor's badge and went inside the office. The D&Y office was pretty much like any other office, cubicles in rows and columns, with meeting rooms at the far corners. My eyes were searching for Priya; I could not find her.

We reached Suhana's cabin. Meanwhile, Ritesh came in with a coffee mug. 'Care for a coffee?' Ritesh asked.

'No thanks, I am just coming from a meeting. Had my dose of it in the morning,' I replied.

'As you wish.' He dragged another chair and made himself comfortable.

'What brings you here?' asked Ritesh.

'I have received your email where you have essentially refused to alter the evaluation criteria. Don't get me wrong, but by doing so you are actually limiting Wiretech Insys, one of the world's biggest and leading networking solution-providing companies to participate in the country's biggest networking project. Should we read this as a deliberate attempt to not allow us to quote in this project? And is this attempt, we dare say, influenced by our competition?' I hit them below the belt in the sweetest manner possible.

Suhana tried to say something, but Ritesh stopped her and began addressing my concerns. 'I understand, Atul. If I had been in your position, I would have also reacted in this manner. But try and understand that these decisions are not driven by personal choices. We have a team of experts who evaluate and approve each and every proposal. In your case, we had a detailed debate on the points raised by you, but unfortunately, the decision was taken collectively.'

'Oh, come on, Ritesh. I also work in an organization and I, too, have my set of approvers, but I know how to get a particular bit of work done. I am sure since you guys are driving this case, you would know how to get this done. Help me, guys. This is big for me.' I deliberately placed my hands on Ritesh's knee to make him feel as if I was ready to touch his feet.

He was moved by the gesture. 'It's almost over from our end. We had a discussion on this. But if you can convince Priya Arya, maybe she can do something.'

I always knew it, bugger, but I wanted you to be on my side too.

'That will be so nice of you. Tell me how I should proceed?' I sounded like an excited child.

'She is busy all day in meetings. I don't know whether she can spare some time for you,' Suhana said.

'No worries, I will catch her and talk to her. I am sure if you guys support me, it will be smooth sailing for me.' Ritesh and Suhana smiled. I had made them feel important. I wished them goodbye and moved towards the reception area. Just when I was about to leave, I saw Priya coming out of a cabin. She had seen me walking out of the door. I called her from my hand phone; she did not pick up. I sent her a text: I am waiting for you in the lobby on the ground floor of the building. Will not leave without meeting you.

~

I waited outside in the lobby till the evening, smoking a cigarette every forty-five minutes. At around 6.30 p.m., she came out of the lift. She was with her colleagues. Our eyes met briefly before she turned her gaze and passed me without saying a word.

Oh God, I missed an opportunity to have a word with her. What should I do? Should I go to her hotel and wait for her there?

I was lost in thought when someone tapped my back.

'Hi, Priya,' I smiled.

'We can't talk here. There are a lot of office colleagues around. Follow me to the food court in the other building,' Priya said.

I followed Priya like an obedient child. She found a lonely corner in the huge food court and sat there. I went to the nearby Subway outlet and bought two Veggie Delite subs and orange juice. *It's evening and she must be hungry. And above all, serious conversations cannot be digested on an empty stomach.*

'This is for you. Have it. It must have been a long day. This is veg with no cheese and no calories.' I placed the sandwich in front of her. Priya was flabbergasted at my ever-so-normal behaviour.

'Thanks,' she opened it and took a bite.

'This reminds me of Bhopal,' I said while digging into the sumptuous sandwich. She was quiet.

'I miss the lakes here. It is a sea of big cars and people roaming endlessly from one corner of the city to another,' I dropped another line. She did not pay attention to anything I had to say. I let her finish her sandwich and drink the orange juice.

Now was the right time.

'After that brief encounter with Charu, I did not ever speak to her. It was a rare slip from my side. I was a kid at that time, Priya. Don't punish me for that. If you will not forgive me, I will die. I could not get into any other relationship after you. Every day and night, I think only about you. Now that you have come back, I will not let you go. Don't do this to me, Priya. I love you, I really love you.' I placed my hands on hers.

Priya listened to my words quietly. She closed her eyes and by the time she opened them, they were considerably wet. 'I want to believe you Atul. But I can't. Like you, I also carried that wound deep in my heart and it has still not healed. I need time. As I said, I am seeing someone. I can't inflict the same pain on him.'

My vision blurred as tears came into my eyes. 'Priya, I don't know about anyone else, but I can't leave you now, and I promise I shall love you forever. Please come back to me.'

I held both her hands and we sat like that for a couple of minutes. Priya slowly dragged her hands back and wiped her eyes with her handkerchief. She got up, put her bag over her shoulder and walked away. All of a sudden, she turned back. 'Atul, I can't help you with the tender. It's beyond my limits.'

'This is not about anything else, Priya. This is about love.'

She turned again and started walking towards the exit. I stood there and kept looking at her. I lit a cigarette and walked towards the car parking. As I drove towards my home that night, I decided I would go to Sushil Rajput and tell him I could not do this any more. He had to accept my failure. All I wanted now was Priya.

Day 4

The next day I sent an SMS to Sushil Rajput, requesting him to take some time out to meet me. Although his doors were always open to his colleagues, it was more than evident that he liked it when they were more formal, more obedient towards him.

I drove from NOIDA to Gurgaon and reached office an

hour before the meeting. Throughout the journey, I kept rehearsing my discussion with Sushil. I wanted to choose my words carefully to ensure that nothing went terribly wrong. I wanted him to understand that this was not my failure, and that one cannot control matters of the heart.

At 1.45 p.m., I entered Sushil's cabin. I sat on the seat in front of him.

'Yes, tell me now.'

'Sir, I have always treated you as my elder brother and as a leader I look up to. I have a dream in life, sir, to become like you. But I am stuck, and I have taken a decision. I wanted to share it with you.'

'What happened?' he tried to make me feel comfortable.

In the next half-an-hour, I told Sushil Rajput about my twisted love story with Priya and how I saw myself as a pawn in God's great game of destiny. I kept talking and during my entire narration, Sushil kept quiet and stared at me. His right fist was kept below his chin just like the sculpture of Rodin the Thinker. I finished the narration with the enthusiasm of a kid and the zest of a lover. I looked helplessly at Sushil, hoping he would set me free.

'Finished?' he asked.

'Yes, sir,' I said in a low voice.

'Do you know what you are talking about?' he asked casually.

'Yes, sir.'

He stood up, walked slowly towards me and sat in front of me on the table.

'Stop being a kid, Mr Atul Shukla. Do you have any idea what the fuck you are going to do? For God's sake, this is not a weekend squash game where you get up in between and say,

"Hey guys, I gotta go." This is a matter of your career and it's not only about your career, it's about my career too. Our lives are dependent on this and I cannot let a novice fuck my life and go just because he cannot handle his ex-girlfriend, because he cannot break her heart once again, because he cannot win her over.'

I had anticipated his outburst, but not its intensity.

Sushil bent towards me and placed his hands over my shoulders and said, 'This is a big game and you are already in it. A token of ₹75 lakh has already been paid to the mantriji by Chaurasia and if we back out now, who will bear the loss?' I looked at Sushil with my eyes wide open. This was not only Chaurasia's money, it was Sushil's money too, and the way he said the last line 'who will bear the loss?' exposed him completely. If I were to back out now, he would surely come after me.

For a second I wanted to defy him. But then I reminded myself that I had spent nearly eight years in the company and a lot of sweat and blood had gone into achieving everything that I had today. Even if I was to look for a job elsewhere, I would have to prove myself all over again. My position was very similar to Arjuna's in the battlefield. He had Lord Krishna to enlighten him; I had Sushil Rajput.

Guessing my state of mind, Sushil put a hand on my shoulders. 'Listen, Atul, I am telling you one last time. Only two days are left before the final recommendations are submitted by the consultants. You must try, either by hook or by crook, to get those recommendations in our favour. And I know my champ can do this, just apply yourself. This is a testing time and if you overcome this, you will conquer the world; if you run away in between, then no one except you yourself will be responsible for your failure.'

A lot was hidden in Sushil Rajput's words. In some ways, Priya had already rejected me. The only way she could help me now was to facilitate the process of passing the tender. Whether I liked it or not, I had to make her do it. I had to win her heart only to break it all over again. I got up from the chair and looked into Sushil's eyes.

'I will do it, sir.'

'That's like my boy.'

I marched out of Sushil's cabin like a dogged soldier who was ready to kill or be killed. I headed straight towards Priya's office. She was my only chance now; I needed to know who would take the decision in her organization. I didn't know anybody higher than her in D&Y. Suhana and Ritesh were junior to her and I didn't have enough time to find a new senior person in the organization. Priya was my best chance, but she was also my biggest obstacle.

At the D&Y office, I didn't call Priya. Instead I waited outside her building's exit. At around 6.30 p.m., Priya came out of the lift.

'Hi Priya, this is not Bangalore. Winter can be very hard in this part of the country.'

'I know, but offices are usually warm.' Priya did not look surprised to see me.

'There are some good malls here with great eating joints. Do you mind if we have dinner together, maybe a movie, and then I'll drop you back at the hotel? I don't know what all this will lead to, but while you are here, let's spend some time together.'

She gave me a mischievous smile.

She knows my ways, doesn't she?

'It seems reasonably fine. I have a friend of mine, do you

mind if I call...'

'No problem, you can call her.'

'Varun...' She turned around and looked at a guy standing slightly away from her and gestured to him to come to her. It seemed that Priya had asked him to wait for her. Varun was a tall, handsome man in his early thirties. He was wearing a long winter coat, with a white shirt and black tie. His head was covered with thick wavy hair. He was a character straight out of a typical Mills and Boon novel.

'Varun, meet Atul, a friend from my college days. He has invited us for dinner and a movie this evening. What do you say?'

My personal dating request was an invitation for 'us'.

'Yeah, that sounds great,' instant acceptance came from Varun in a thick accent. 'Let me call for the car.' I looked at him in envy, why must he be a typical third guy in a typical Bollywood love triangle—charming, suave and genuinely nice?

'He is a chikna. Where did you find him?' I whispered in Priya's ears.

'I did not find him. He works with me in my company.' Her childlike reply made me laugh and she was amused to see my reaction.

'Are you seeing this guy?' She nodded her head slowly. I was shocked and surprised.

'He is good, but...you know, I never knew you would like somebody like him...somebody...so perfect.'

'Why? What's the problem with him?' she kept her hands on her hips as if I had disliked a new dress of a twelve-year-old girl and she was offended. For a moment, the business woman in her was gone and my Priya was back. I looked at her eyes and smiled, 'I will get my car.'

We reached Ambience Mall in Gurgaon. Priya went in Varun's car. The ride was not very long, but I kept on thinking about her. I was overwhelmed by a feeling of jealousy. I was a greenhorn compared to Varun, but then why was I even comparing myself with him? Priya's relationship with me needed time to grow and I didn't have it. She was seeing someone else. If I needed Priya back in my life, I had to sacrifice my job and future. But at the same time, I wanted to preserve everything I had achieved so far in life at the cost of my values and love. Well, who does not make sacrifices?

'Lots of good-looking people here,' came a man-to-man one-liner from me, referring obviously to the beautiful women in the food court in the mall. Varun, too, was looking around. Priya was not amused, she gave us that familiar men-will-be-men look. A couple of good-looking girls went past us. Varun looked at them and remarked casually, 'Delhi guys really wear their attitude on their sleeves. I was born and brought up in Hyderabad and whenever I come to Delhi, I cannot stop admiring its beauty and, of course, the beauties.'

Priya looked at Varun in surprise.

'And what about people who do not have a sleeve to wear their attitude on?' I pointed towards a girl wearing a sleeveless top. Varun looked at her and both of us broke into laughter.

'Stop this nonsense, you cheapo,' Priya punched me on my back, dragged me away from Varun and stood between us like a protective mom. 'Let's go to the restaurant now.'

Varun kept laughing and I looked at her eyes. This was the first time she had touched me on her own and expressed herself without any inhibitions.

The ice is melting slowly.

We went to the restaurant Punjab Grill, which had topped the *Times Food Guide* list several times. We ordered some authentic tandoori and Punjabi dishes along with some whisky and a mocktail for the lady. I expected Priya to order some vodka, but she was still a non-smoking, non-drinking, ethical girl with high values.

Varun wanted to pay heed to his Punjabi mannerisms and so he ordered chicken and some large pegs of whisky. I did not pay much attention to his elaborate description of love between kukkad (chicken) and Delhi. I was only interested in finding out how D&Y operated.

'It must be fun being into consulting, isn't it?' I asked Varun.

'At times it is. At times it is not,' he replied, sipping his drink.

'Well, there's a flipside to everything in life, but I am really curious how you guys are structured.' We gulped one large Johnnie Walker Black Label on the rocks each and I ordered a repeat of the drinks along with some kukkads. Varun, by now, was at ease with me and he started his quick tour of the consultancy business.

'I will try not to sound like one of our client presentations or straight out of our company webpage but to describe in a nutshell, consultancy is basically of two types—one is audit-related, how have you done, and the other is advisory, how to do. At D&Y, we deal with both the types of consultancies and charge our customers on the basis of the services we provide. They are corporates, the government and those from the education sector. For the government, we only do advisory contracts, which can be of various types like a government's system study, delivery of programmes within time and a budget and providing consulting services to the government on tenders, process management, best practices, and so on. We bid for the project and once through, we sign the agreement with the government.'

The fact that Priya had introduced me as her college friend was helping as Varun did not think sharing this information with a complete outsider was a big deal.

'What is your role?' I asked.

'I am the associate director,' he replied.

He holds a prominent position in the organization.

Before Varun enquired about my role, I quickly changed the topic. 'Let's take one more,' I pointed toward his empty glass. The waiter dutifully filled our glasses.

In the meantime, Priya was giving us another men-will-be-men look. We ordered some dahi kebabs and a virgin mojito for her. She looked disgusted at the way Varun and I were getting along. She did not expect that; she wanted me to be jealous and had deliberately got Varun along with her. She wanted to send across the message that it was over between us. But for me, it had just begun. I had not given a single hint of jealousy and was acting my part of being perfectly normal and casual all evening. She, too, joined in the conversation.

'We appoint consultants for each client and then there are senior consultants and managers and senior managers supervising them. Varun is our boss in that sense,' Priya smiled and looked at Varun, who was enjoying his scotch.

'Great, you are the boss, so you must be taking all the decisions? That's cool,' I wanted to get a clearer idea of the organization's hierarchy.

'Nothing really,' Varun shrugged it off with an air of casualness and taking refuge in the modern mantra of management by empowerment, he continued, 'The primary decision on any matter is by the consultant responsible, but for some major clients or big projects, we make a committee of experts on the issue and then reach a joint conclusion.'

So had Priya decided in my favour, the complications could have been avoided. She should have been able to solve it at her level, but her non-diluting, rock-solid values did not allow her to do so and so she had referred the case to the committee, which had taken a decision against us because of obvious reasons—we were indeed trying to dilute the quality standards.

I kept them engaged in the ever-generic topics of the IT landscape in the country, the growing economy, the damning recession, Bollywood versus Hollywood. Dinner was followed by a late night show of a Hollywood blockbuster at a nearby multiplex. Varun could not hold on to the large pegs of scotch he had had and soon the dialogues in the film were obliterated by his snores. His head fell backward and he slept with his mouth wide open. Priya was embarrassed and tried to shake him, but Varun had passed out.

We finished the movie without speaking a word. Priya was careful to maintain a substantial distance from me throughout the film. We slowly strolled towards our car. Varun was half asleep.

'Do you mind if I drop the lady to her hotel?'

Varun looked at Priya; she was befuddled.

'Is the hotel on your way?' asked Varun.

I had to go to Noida, which was in the opposite direction and at least an hour's drive from there, 'It hardly matters, we have met after a long time,' I insisted. Somehow or the other, Priya kept away from the discussion—maybe she wanted the best man to win.

'Cool,' Varun withdrew himself.

For the first time ever, Priya was sitting alongside me on the front seat of my car. We both kept quiet for a while, I wanted the feeling of togetherness to sink into both of us. I deliberately drove slowly; it was late in the night, and was cold. Priya folded her arms across her chest, I tried to hand over my jacket to her but she refused to take it.

'You did not stop me from driving you back to the hotel?' I broke the silence.

'I knew you could not be stopped. It's better to let you do what you want to do for the next two days and then leave.' I wasn't sure what was colder—the weather or Priya's response.

I stopped the car under the porch of the Crowne Plaza Hotel. Priya stepped out.

'Won't you ask me for a cup of coffee?'

She turned around, looked at me and smiled, 'You will not change, Atul Shukla. Come.'

Hassi toh phasi, part II.

We walked together across the corridor and inside the lift. A strange feeling crept inside me. After so many years we were together—I wanted to hold her and kiss her passionately, but then I knew I was walking a tight rope.

The coffee shop was closed and Priya invited me to her room. I was not sure what was going on in her mind but being alone with her at night was being too close to the fire. We entered the room, and I sat on the sofa. I took the water bottle and fed some water to my alcohol-drenched body.

'How are your mom and little sis?' I asked her.

She gave me a curious look, perhaps wondering why sex

was not the first thing on my mind.

'They are fine. Mummy stays with me in Bangalore and the kiddo is preparing for CA in Pune.' She made herself comfortable on the bed, placing a pillow on her thighs and letting her arms lean on it.

Is she testing me?

'Great, your hard work paid off. You are a strong lady.' She didn't say anything, just smiled.

'I will get some coffee for you.' She got up and started preparing the coffee. As soon as she was done, Priya handed over the cup to me.

'Wow, it's great.' Once again, she preferred to remain silent.

Her BlackBerry beeped and she looked at the handset, 'Oh shit, I forgot to send a mail. Excuse me, I need to send it now.' She got up and took her laptop out of the bag. I looked at her. She opened the machine, typed a password and started working on the machine. I kept sipping the hot coffee. She was done with her work in five minutes.

'Sorry,' she took the coffee cup and sipped, 'This was urgent. It was a mail from the management. I had to complete the final draft of the tender document and send it back to the client.' My heart sank. Had she completed it and sent it? I pretended being absolutely dispassionate about the tender.

'Are you done with it?' I asked in a casual tone.

'Almost, some minor work is left. Anyway, I have two more days to respond to them. I had to send some documents to my boss. He is in the US, that's why I rushed to the laptop.'

She said she had some more work to do. What could that be?

'I am sorry, Atul. I could not help your company in this tender. Your requests were unjustified and I cannot dilute the qualifying criteria. Moreover, the contract between our company and the Himachal government has a stamp from the Ministry of Law. This is too important a project for us to mess up.' She had said it so easily. I felt drugged. I wanted to hold her and shake her, but decided against it.

Once again, I tried hard to conceal my true feelings. 'It's okay, Priya, I understand and appreciate your commitment to the quality of your work. I am used to defeats now. I could not get you; I could not get this once-in-a-lifetime tender.' I stood up and placed the empty cup on the table.

'Thanks for the coffee. As I said, our relationship is beyond any tender or any such trivial thing. You will be leaving soon, and I cannot have enough of you and will come for more. Thank you for this evening and good night. Take care.' I walked in the lobby towards the elevator. I could sense her walking up to the door and watching me leave.

I sat in my car, and looked for the half-empty vodka bottle below the back seat. It had already been a drunken evening, but I wanted a deep sleep tonight. It was a long drive back home to Noida. It was 12.02 a.m. I bought a cola bottle from one of the midnight parathewalas outside one of the call centres. As I drove back drinking, I was still not sure of my next move. But if I knew Priya well, my sentimentalization of her role in the tender allocation would most likely yield positive results.

DAY 5

I am running. Running hard and fast. I hear the sound of dry leaves crushing under my feet. Somebody, I sense, is chasing me and I need to hide myself. I slip behind the boundary wall of a dark well and hide myself. The sound of footsteps intensifies and then fades. I slowly get up to go home. My mother is waiting for me, but I see a big wall in front of me. I turn towards my left, the wall is also there. I turn towards my right, there it is again. I am thirsty. I am tired. And I am stuck.

I got up with a jolt, rubbed my eyes repeatedly to ensure it was a dream. I could not remember if I had slept last night. I had tossed and turned trying to figure out what the hell I was doing with my life. Should I resign? Should I beg Priya to help me? She was leaving in two days and would be submitting the final report any time now. I had no time left.

In this grand corporate battle, I was merely a foot-soldier whose sacrifices will never be accounted for. If this deal fell through, the money Chaurasia and Sushil had paid to the minister would not come back to them. At best, the minister would promise them another favour in another deal in the near future. Knowing Sushil, he would seethe in rage and would make me the scapegoat. On the other hand, I did not know what was happening in Priya's mind. My relationship with her had lasted only for a week, but the bond I had formed with her was strong. Was this deal worth breaking her heart, above all, breaking her spirit forever?

I picked up my mobile phone only to realize that there were a number of missed calls, one from Sushil too. I cursed myself for giving him the impression that I could *always* get the work done. I did not have the energy to talk to him, so I decided to do the next best thing:

'Work in progress. Will update you by evening,' I typed a text message and sent it to him. He did not reply, which seemed unusual. His silence spoke a thousand words. I had to rush to Priya's office and see what was happening. I quickly ate my lunch, dressed in a dark grey Louis Philippe business suit and sprayed Hugo Boss on, hoping its fragrance would change the course of events.

I drove towards Gurgaon and by the time I reached, it was around 4.45 p.m. It was foggy, and later I came to know it was the coldest day of winter that year. My phone rang; Veeru was calling me. My instinct was to pick up the phone and pour my heart out to him, but I decided against it. I parked my car and lit a cigarette. My phone rang again. This time, it was Mitali Bagga, the HR head.

Are they already hunting me?

'Hi,' I took her call.

'Where have you been? I did not see you at work for the last couple of days,' Mitali asked me.

'I was busy with a project.'

'When will you be back? Are you travelling?'

'No, it will be finished in two days,' I replied.

'See you then.' She hung up.

I called Priya's mobile number. She did not take the call. As soon as I finished another cigarette, my phone rang again. It was Priya.

Thank God.

I wanted to answer it immediately, but then did not want to give an impression that I was too keen. I waited for a few seconds, let the phone ring for some time and then picked up.

'Hi Atul, my phone was in silent mode. Tell me.'

'What can I tell you? I am downstairs, when can we meet?' I was gripped by a childlike enthusiasm.

'I am stuck at work and shall be free after an hour. I don't know whether we can meet today.'

She might be completing the SWAAN tender.

'Oh come on, you know me. I will not leave while you are here. Please let me spend as much time with you as possible. I can come upstairs and wait for you.' I wanted to check what exactly she was doing.

'That won't look good, Atul. Wait for me downstairs. I will come in an hour.'

My offer was turned down. I had no option but to wait for her. She was at least ready to meet me and after a long time, she had referred to me as Atul and not 'Mr Atul Shukla'.

Was this a positive sign?

I went to the nearby coffee shop to pass time. After an hour, she came downstairs and I met her just outside the lobby. Thankfully, she was alone.

'So, where will you take me today?' she said, folding her arms around her chest with a sparkle in her eyes.

'There are no lakes here. The streets are full of traffic, so no long drive. This place has a hell of a lot of good eating joints. I can take you to one of them.'

'I have left my laptop in the office. I have something to wind up, so you drop me here later.'

No midnight coffee today?

'Sure.'

We reached Jolly Rogers on MG Road. It's a swanky, rooftop restaurant. A small candle was lit on the table. Priya had by now succumbed to the cold weather of north India and was in multiple layers of winter clothing. Wrapped in a long-necked sweater, she was looking stunning in the dim light of the candle. I now understood why candlelight dinners are supposed to be so romantic. I ordered white rum for myself and a mocktail for Priya.

'Can't you live without drinking one day?' she asked me with an air of authority that suggested that she had some right over me.

'Nasha has become a part of my life now. I don't want to get out of this.'

'Oh come on, don't give me this Devdas stuff. It's too filmy. The fact is you should get married now and settle down in life. Excessive drinking is bad for health.'

Preacher Priya.

'Whoever said married men don't drink? I don't drink out of any compulsion or frustration. Who knows, if I marry the wrong girl I might start drinking even more.' My emphasis on wrong girl embarrassed her slightly.

'Why don't you get married?' It was my turn now.

'I don't know.'

We kept quiet for some time, behaving like strangers in the middle of people chatting and enjoying themselves.

'Priya, let me acknowledge this in front of you today. You are a brave girl. What you have made out of your life is nothing short of being great. I am really happy and proud of you.'

She closed her eyes and smiled, as if to let the words sink in. She opened her eyes and with a look of belongingness in her eyes, said, 'I am also very happy for you, Atul. I am sure your parents are proud of you.'

'Yeah, they are happy and proud and want me to settle down soon. I also don't know why I don't want to settle in life. I just wonder if we will be happier being together.' I finished my drink and placed the glass on the table.

Priya kept quiet. She obviously didn't have an answer to my question.

'So you are done with your work here?' I started again.

'Almost. I will be leaving tomorrow evening. I had to send the final report to the client and they will then begin work on it.'

She has still not sent the file.

'My team and Varun have compiled the work. Once Varun appraises the report for our US office, we will send it to the client.' She updated me, one by one, on her company's approval process and all of them were over by now. The final tender document was ready to be presented to the customer. As I heard it from Priya, all my hopes were crushed. Suddenly the liquor stopped working and I ordered some more large pegs.

'I know, Atul, that was a big deal for you, but I really can't help you.'

'You don't have to be sorry about that. In fact, I am happy that because of this project I got to spend time with you.'

We finished dinner reminiscing about our good old days in Bhopal. The beauty of the city, the carelessness we revelled in when we were young, our first meeting, our shyness, our desires. I drove Priya back to the office. As she got down, my instinct was to hold her tight and shake her, saying, 'IF YOU DON'T DO WHAT I SAY, I WILL BE FUCKED!'

A group of people had gathered around the office entrance. It was 9 p.m. and two cab drivers had picked up a fight, leading to a gathering of curious onlookers. A big cluster of vehicles had formed around the area, a mini traffic jam. We had to take a U-turn to reach the place. I stopped the vehicle on the other side of the road. 'Shit, looks like it will get worse now,' I said.

'Damn! I should have got the laptop with me in the first place.'

'You have some work to complete?' I asked.

'No, I just have to send a mail. That's it.'

'You can do it in the hotel. I will drop you there. Let me get the laptop for you. Give me your access card. It's not good for you to go on the other side of the road.'

She handed over her ID card, which also served as an electronic access card for the employees.

'Sixth floor, seat number M-146, on the right corner, just plug it out and take it for me,' Priya instructed.

I leapt across the road and the elevator took me to the sixth floor. I walked towards the reception and did not tell the security guard that I was a visitor. Instead, I pretended to be an employee, for a visitor had to be accompanied by an escort from the D&Y group. I walked towards the gate confidently with the ID card in my hand, which was not clearly visible to the guards. As I flashed my card in front of the sensor, one of the guards stopped me.

'Excuse me, sir.'

My heart sank for a second. 'What's it?' I asked with considerable authority to give an impression that he was stopping me from doing something urgent and important.

'Sir, please make an entry in the register,' the guard was pointing towards the employee register. Without any further delay, I quickly signed the register with a bogus signature and entered the working area. I took a right turn inside and kept walking. I reached M-146 and saw Priya's laptop in sleep mode. I looked at the machine and felt like a poor man standing in front of a locker with riches inside.

The final report must be on the laptop.

I don't know what propelled me but I switched on the laptop. The initial MS Windows screen flashed; it instructed me to press *ctrl+alt+del*. I pressed the three keys together, the next window asked for a password.

'Shit, that's a dead end,' I whispered to myself. For a second, I thought of giving up and taking the laptop to Priya as promised. But the next moment I found myself looking around. Nobody was there. I tried guessing the password.

'Priya621983'

It is Priya's birthday.

I typed it.

Enter.

'The password or user name you are trying is incorrect.'

The laptop would give me only three chances.

'Welcome2012'

Passwords are usually lame.

I typed it.

Enter.

'The password or user name you are trying is incorrect.'

SHIT! Only one chance left now!

I was thinking hard. My phone rang; its loud noise felt like a warning from God. I picked it up, it was Priya.

'Could you get it?'

'I have it. I am on my way back, waiting for the lift,' I lied.

I don't have much time.

My drunken mind was concentrating hard on the patterns Priya's fingers were following when she logged into her system last night. I tried hard to think of all the possible words, phrases, numbers and the combination of all these that she could have chosen for a password. And finally, I zeroed in on one.

'Cutiepie83'

This was her email address a long time ago. I took a deep

breath, closed my eyes and typed it.

Enter.

BINGO

The system accepted the password and I patted myself on the back.

As soon as the desktop icons emerged, I clicked on 'My Documents'. Amid an array of documents with incongruous titles, I found 'SWAAN RFP Final.doc'.

This should be the one.

I began reading it quickly. It was the final format of the tender. The list reflected twelve points. It had two points, on quality certifications and experience of working in India. I decided to edit it, change it the way I wanted Priya to. I added the phrase 'or similar projects outside India' to the sentence, making it 'experience of working in India or similar projects outside India'. I now turned towards the qualification criteria and added the phrase 'or any other equivalent US standards'. The complete sentence now indicated that any company that had European and US quality standards was eligible to quote. The remarks column read, 'The executive committee after discussing the representations from the vendors and after due diligence on each point has concluded on the above mentioned qualification criteria.'

I saved and closed the file. I quickly searched for any file pertaining to recommendations and observations. My attention was caught by 'Response to the Queries.doc'. I double clicked on the file—it had a description of the key deliverables for project SWAAN.

I read quickly and reached the page that had a table mentioning all the points raised by various vendors. I scrolled down towards the column that mentioned Wiretech Insys. The remarks column read:

'The issues raised by M/s Wiretech Insys: After due diligence by the executive team it has decided not to approve it.'

I deleted the word 'not' from the column, giving it a completely new meaning. I quickly searched for any other remarks that could ruin our chances, but could not find one. Blood was flowing rather rapidly in my veins. I could barely control my hands from trembling. Finally, my work was done. All I now had to do was to ensure that Priya did not look at the file carefully before sending it.

I shut down the laptop and quickly kept it inside the bag. As I was stuffing the laptop inside the box, my eyes went to an old diary kept in a corner of the desk. It had the words 'MY D' scribbled on it with a sketch pen. I remembered Priya once standing by me on the lakeside in Bhopal saying, 'I was talking to MY D the whole night.' When I had asked her who 'MY D' was, she had said, 'She is my best friend.'

It was Priya's personal diary. Since this was a night of breaking all the rules, I decided to keep it. I zipped the laptop bag and was walked briskly towards the door.

'Hey!' a sound hit me like an arrow. I was shocked. I looked towards the direction of the voice.

It was Varun. 'Hi, Varun,' my face reflected a nervous smile. He was equally surprised. Varun first stared at me with suspicion and then looked at Priya's laptop.

'I came to pick Priya's laptop.' I gave a nervous reply.

He was not amused. It was evident that he did not appreciate a stranger walking into the office with a colleague's laptop that could possibly have important documents. Luckily for me, my phone rang and it was Priya asking me what was taking me so long.

'Hey Priya, I met Varun upstairs. Coming in two minutes.' I turned towards Varun and said, 'Sorry bro, need to rush. Will catch up with you later.' I came back jogging towards the car; the jam was slowly getting over now. I kept the laptop on the back seat.

'I bumped into Varun,' I casually tried to explain my delay.

'I should not have sent you. It is against our security policies, and Varun might not have felt particularly good about it.' Priya seemed worried.

'Oh come on, tell him you could not come because of the scene outside and I am sure Varun will understand.' In the meantime, her mobile phone rang. As she had predicted, it was Varun complaining about why she had sent me to the office unaccompanied. I could hear Priya explaining the situation to him and finally saying, 'Yes, okay, fine, absolutely, immediately.' By the time she had finished, we had reached her hotel.

It was time to say goodbye. She was leaving the next day and our tryst with destiny was coming to an end.

'A final coffee...perhaps?' I asked.

She refused, got down from the car and started walking towards the huge entrance gate. I looked at her going away. My heart was pounding. I had to ensure that Priya sent the mail without looking at the changes I had made. I did not want to leave her now. At that moment, she stopped, turned around and walked towards me. 'For the last time,' she said.

I gave the car keys to the valet and we both walked side by side once again towards the lift. For the first time in these five days, she initiated a conversation.

'It was nice spending time with you, Atul. At least we got to know each other's perspective.'

'We are still not done. A lot can happen over coffee, my dear.'

We reached her room and since we were alone, desires began to take precedence in my head. Priya seemed awkward too. The situation was far too dangerous for both of us. I sat on the sofa again. 'What did Varun say?' I deliberately started the conversation.

'Nothing, he briefed me about the go ahead he had received from our US office. He had just finished the conference call with them when he saw you coming from my desk.' I shook my head as if I appreciated the gravity of the situation.

'Then what's the next step?'

'I need to mail the client and then it's all finished from our side.' She moved her shoulders casually, handed the coffee cup to me and sat on the bed with a pillow on her lap.

'Why don't you send the mail and finish today's job?' I suggested. I could not afford the chance of her looking at the file tomorrow and noticing the changes.

'Hmm, I want to spend time with you,' she said.

Surprise, surprise!

'I have time till this coffee lasts. If you work on the laptop, I will have time till your work finishes.' My words did not seem to have any effect on her; she did not budge. I sipped the last of my coffee and put the cup back on the table. At that moment, she looked at me and smiled. She got up and opened her laptop.

Bingo! I have to divert her attention now.

'Where do we go from here?' I asked.

My question caught her off guard. She looked at me as

if she was standing between two worlds. I kept staring at her.

'I don't know.' That's not what I had expected. Her laptop was on by then and she typed the password. For a second, I feared a message…

'Your laptop has been logged in by an unknown user and data has been tampered with.'

Thankfully, this facility is yet to be invented.

'I know I will go nowhere from here. After meeting you, all I can say is that I can die peacefully now. I will never be able to get into another relationship now,' I once again tried to engage her in talk.

I could sense her opening various programmes and clicking on different keys. I deliberately switched the TV on and kept changing channels.

'Shit!' she screamed.

'What?'

'The internet connection is not getting through,' she pointed towards the data card on her laptop.

No, not this, please.

'Restart it once,' I suggested.

She restarted the system and was able to access the Internet. 'Oh, it's working now.' She sunk herself in the laptop and I could hear her clicking the keys. I was imagining the file being attached and being sent, a confirmation for which came later.

'It's done,' said Priya.

These words had a healing impact on me. From being nervous, I was ready to jump with joy and call Sushil Rajput and inform him about my newest triumph.

'With this your time ends now. Sorry to say, Mr Atul Shukla, you have not won anything in this episode,' I mimicked Amitabh

Bachchan from *Kaun Banega Crorepati*.

I slowly got up and held Priya's hand. 'Whatever has happened will remain the sweetest memory in my life. You were the most precious gift I could have had in my life, Priya. I love you.' I kissed her palm and walked towards the door. She followed me. I turned back and was about to raise my hand to say goodbye when she grabbed me by my collar, pulled me towards her and kissed me passionately.

'You have not lost anything, Mr Atul Shukla. You have won the jackpot. I love you too.' She smiled and closed the door on my face.

I stood motionless for a moment. I could not believe what was happening to me. Destiny had set everything right. I was on my way to becoming the country manager and had Priya as the interest on the investment. I turned to check if Priya was looking at me, but the door was shut.

I ran towards my car and called up Sushil. After four rings, he picked up.

'Yes, bachche.'

'Boss, it's done. The consultant Priya Arya has sent the final recommendation mail to the customer accepting our conditions.'

'That's like my boy. Very well done. Where are you now?'

'That's a long story. I will tell you tomorrow. Meanwhile, you can give the heads up to Chaurasiaji and ask him to ensure there is no other panga.' It was my time to be demanding.

'Absolutely, mere sher. Take care and see you in the morning.'

I drove the car to the nearby liquor shop. It was still not that late and I got an Absolut vodka bottle for myself from the nearby theka. I mixed it with lime cordial and headed homewards. It was a day of triumphs, and I wanted to end it by getting to know Priya's diary.

13

Priya's Diary

1 January 1996

Dear Diary,

I am sooooo happy Papa bought you for me. He told me writing on your pages is a good habit. It increases my grasp on English. I am in Class IX and this year I will study for the boards. My resolution is to stand first. I will top, na?

24 April 1996

Dear Diary,

I had a fight with Ruchi today. She is so foolish, keeps running after Abhinav. I told her people will start calling her despo. But she does not listen to me. I told her I saw Abhinav on a bike with boys who were wearing earrings. They were also passing bad comments about girls on the road. I am worried about her. God, please save her.

18 August 1996

Dear Diary,

I am studying in a new school now. I feel like crying coz I will not sit with Ruchi any more. I liked my old school. Mummy says Papa is ill and he has to change the job, that's why we are in this new school now. We could not pay the fees in my old school. Pooja is very small. She is always happy playing and does not understand what is happening. I want to cry but Mummy and Papa will feel bad. But I can cry in front of you.

5 December 1996

Dear Diary,

Soooo sorry. I could not write much. I met a boy, his name is Ashish. He is so kind, he gives me notes when I miss classes. These days, I am home most of the time coz Papa is ill. Mummy has joined a new school as a teacher, so she cannot take chutti. I get absent so that I can look after Papa. Papa is very weak. God, pleaseeee make him fine. I promise I will drink milk every day and oil my hair forever.

I almost dreaded flipping the pages now lest there was a confession of true love. What if she had kissed him? I got goose bumps at the very thought of an adolescent Priya kissing a young, faceless boy. When the devil in my mind began to plant negative thoughts, the angel in me began to reassure. If I could have a relationship with Radhika, why wasn't she entitled to have one at such a young age? After all, she is as much of a human being with flesh and blood as I am.

20 March 1997

Dear Diary,

I am afraid. My exams are about to start and I have not been able to study much. Papa is very, very unwell. I heard Mummy weeping in front of Rashmi Aunty. She was saying Papa has cancer and we do not have enough money to spend on him. I felt sooo bad. I went to Mummy at night and told her I do not want to go to school and she can save money for Papa's health. But she said Papa wants me to be a smart lady when I grow up, and if I don't go to school I will not be able to become smart and successful. Little Pooja does not understand about Papa's health. She forced me to take her to Ram Lila Maidan. As she was riding jhoolas, her laughter came out. I was very, very happy to see that. I pray to God she remains happy always. Ruchi hasn't called me. Only Ashish calls me sometimes to check if I am studying. I miss my best friend. Why don't you become my best friend?

8 August 1997

Dear D,

I am in Class XII. My result was not good. I could have done so much better. But Papa says I should not look back. He says Class XI is important and that if I continue to work hard, I will get great results. I feel bad for Papa. His health has become worse. He is not able to eat and walk much. Mummy was scolded by her school's principal because she has taken so much leave. She is upset and got even more upset when she heard of Nana's death just a few days back. She wanted to see her Papa one time before they burnt him, but she cannot go because of my Papa and her school. I don't remember Nana much. He had come home long, long back when Mummy gave birth to Pooja and wanted to take us to Punjab. At that time, Jasjeet Mama fought with Papa and said we should never come to Punjab and think they are dead to us. I am sooo scared of death. If all of us have to die, why do we live? I pray to God that no one I love should die.

21 November 1997

My D,

Ashish proposed to me. We had a free period when we were discussing notes on science. He touched my hand and said I love you. His hand was warm and sweaty. I got scared and thought of movies where people kiss and dance after saying I love you. My cycle friend Shreya says he is cute and every girl in the school would be J if he and I became boyfriend and girlfriend. But how can I say I love him when I don't know what love is? Why don't you tell me?

I looked at the clock. It was 3 a.m. I filled my empty glass with some vodka and proceeded.

14 April 2001

My D,

Papa is no more. I cannot tell you what I am going through. Mummy is uncontrollable. Pooja hugged me and cried and cried. I wish I could do that also. But if I cry, Mummy and Pooja will cry even more and feel more helpless. I have to look after both of them now that Papa is gone. I have to be brave during the day. If at all I have to cry, I go to the balcony once Mummy and Pooja have gone to sleep and cry looking at the stars. I am sure Papa

watches me cry every night from the sky. Maybe if
he watches me cry every day, he will come back.

With every tear she shed, Priya also parted with the young,
spirited girl that she was. The measured, confident Priya that
I knew was born the day her father passed away. As I read
about her internal struggle of dealing with her father's death,
I thought of my own parents. In a bid to make it big in life,
I had never spared much thought to what was happening to
them. One odd phone call in a month and I assumed that I
had fulfilled my responsibilities as a son. I was the only child; I
shuddered to think of the hurt my callousness had caused them.
They were, after all, the only people in my life with whom I
did not share a relationship of convenience.

The content of the following pages was heartening. Priya,
it seems, had done particularly well academically—getting in
the merit list, getting a scholarship from a college in Raipur. I
was particularly touched by an episode where Priya expressed
the sheer thrill of getting the scholarship money because she
could help her mother pay Pooja's school fee for the quarter.

It was also evident that Priya's mother had been successful
in inculcating values in her children. What was remarkable was
that she encouraged them to lead their lives as independently as
possible with the condition that they should never compromise
on their self-respect.

Finally, I moved on to the year 2004, when Priya and I had
met on the train. I was nervous at the prospect of reading what
she had felt about me. The first few paragraphs were dedicated
to her excitement of getting into the MBA college in Indore.

29 June 2004

My D,

I was on my way back from Indore when I met this really funny guy on the train. His name is Atul Shukla. He came across a bit weird initially but was cute. He is definitely not the Mills and Boon kind, but there is something very charming and filmy about him. He was trying to be Shah Rukh Khan of *Dilwale Dulhaniya Le Jayenge*, but little does he know I am no Simran ☺

15 July 2004

My D,

Surprise, surprise. I got a mail from Atul. Atul, who? Arrey, that guy straight out of DDLJ, whom I met on the train. He has arranged a small industrial training course for me in Bhopal. Isn't it reallllly nice of him? He has also arranged industrial training for Rakhi. Rakhi has warned me that this is his way of impressing me, but I don't care as long as he is helping me.

21 July 2004

My D,

Atul came to meet me after office. I was kinda expecting that. We went out for a ride to a lake on his bike. It was beautiful, it was green, it was cool, it was breezy. Very romantic it was. There is a certain warmth about Atul and I like that. I wanted to spend some more time, but it was getting late and I had to rush to Rajesh Bhaiyya's place. Anyway too late now, good night.

22 July 2004

D,

So we spent one more evening together. I am unable to sleep now. We went to another lake today, this city is gorgeous. Umm, I don't think I can be just friends with this guy. But then I cannot commit to him. At this point, there's just too much to do, and I cannot afford any distraction. What to do!

23 July 2004

D,

Finalllly, it happened! Atul proposed. I am feeling very excited, though I am scared as well. I told Rakhi about it and she is just as excited. In her opinion, Atul is a good guy. As you know, he is not the first guy to propose to me, but I am yet to meet someone as honest, down-to-earth, committed as Atul. I have not said yes, as no girl should. But I am tempted to. I want to make him wait for a bit and see how patient he is. Meanwhile, let me dance with joy.

You and I
I walked all alone in a lost lane,
danced to my own tune in the first rain,

hummed a melody my heart couldn't sing,
unknown to the smiles true love can bring...

24 July 2004

Yes...I said yes. Atul's friend Ramakant came to meet
me in office and told me he would be leaving the
country soon and wanted to tell me just how much
Atul loved me. Ramakant does not know he brought
me the bestest news of my life. I sooo wish Papa
was alive. Then Atul would have easily become the
son he never had.
Unknown to the smiles true love can bring, true
love can bring.

<u>You and I</u>
Like the first ray of light that ends the night,
my days glowed with your love when you stepped
into my life.
You were the first drop of rain on parched earth,
the seed of love from which life gives birth.

As the wave that dances towards the shore,
my heart leaps now and wants so much more.
Hold my hand and stand by me,
For you and I were meant to be!

25 July 2004

Muah muah kisses love, hugs and kisses, and hug and kisses, and hug and kisses!

26 July 2004

D,
It's over. The most precious moment of my life is over. Atul cheated on me. I feel numb. I do not know what exactly I had done to deserve this. But this is what it is. I loved him, really loved him. Why did he do this? Why, D?

My throat dried and I had tears in my eyes. I should not have taken Priya's diary, but it was a temptation I couldn't have resisted. The following pages indicated how our break-up had transformed her into a gritty corporate woman with a no-nonsense attitude. She cleared her MBA exams with flying colours and got a job with D&Y as part of campus recruitment; she was the only one from her college to be selected by the prestigious company. She shifted base to Bangalore, worked day in and day out, achieving one success after another, getting one promotion after another. I stumbled upon the pages that had her impressions on our second tryst with fate.

19 December 2012

D,

Fate has a strange way of shaking you up just when you think life is going smooth. Remember, Atul? Atul Shukla? The train? The six evenings? He is back, and that too when I am handling a case where I am required to lead the team. He met me in office yesterday. And I am sure he will keep meeting me as long as I am here in Gurgaon. He says he is apologetic about what 'happened' and will always regret it. Do I believe him? I do not know. I am finding myself on a strange plane where professionally, I have to deny him, but personally, I feel drawn to him. Yes, once again. Meeting him made me revisit those memorable six days that have never come back in my life. Will I be able to resist him? Help me, D.

20 December 2012

So Atul took me out on a date, with another man. Shocked? I lied to Atul that I am dating Varun. Strangely, I could not spot any signs of jealousy. Is he genuinely interested in me or has he become a more mature person? I don't know. Anyway, the evening went quite well. I don't remember the last time I had laughed so much. I like the fact that Atul is ready to go the whole mile for me. Let's see where these evenings take us. What say?

Good move, Priya.

21 December 2012

<u>Lonely Heart</u>
As the day adorns a black robe
And the sun turns pale orange
I sit in a corner and relive yesterday
Moments of joy your love would bring.
The smile your thoughts brought on my face
The warmth of melting in your embrace
The time that froze when you looked at me
The love in your eyes only I could see.
The eyes are now empty, the smiles have faded
away
Loneliness swamps my night and day.
I call your name but the voice echoes...
With each passing moment this distance grows.
Come back to me and hold me before I fall,

Reach out to me now and break this wall.
The hope I had nurtured is now dying...
For a love not returned was never mine!

It was the last entry in the diary. I kept reading the last stanza of the poem again and again—*Come back to me and hold me before I fall, come back to me...come back to me...* It was almost 4 a.m. I squeezed myself in one corner of the bed. I had a splitting headache. I held my head with both hands and cried. I cried aloud.

I am not a bad guy Priya. I am not. Please remember that. Always.

14

What is the Correct Path?

I WAS FEELING EMPTY inside and was desperately looking for a friend, philosopher and guide when my heart told my mind, 'Talk to sir, your Guruji.'

Guruji, yes, he could be my guiding light, but in all these years I had not spoken to him, I had never even inquired how he was or where he was. I highly doubted whether he would remember me. I had last spoken to him eight years ago on my birthday and had let his advice go completely unheeded. What had happened? I had lost my best friend and the love of my life.

To call him or not was the dilemma I was in. After pondering over this for quite some time, I decided to go ahead with the call. I took out my cell phone and dialled his number. The line on the other side kept ringing but no one picked up. I tried once again, but there was still no answer. Disappointed, I wiped the tears off my face, placed my head against the wall and closed my eyes.

'I need help.'

'What happened?' Ahmed Ali's face was as radiant as ever.

'Sir, I need your help and guidance.'

'It reminds me of a verse by Kabir: 'Dukh mein sumiran sab kare, sukh mein karena koy, jo sukh mein sumiran kare to dukh kahe ko hoye (Everyone prays in times of suffering, if you pray during good times, suffering will never touch you).'

Ahmed Ali and his riddles. I used to get irritated with them at one point in time, but now I had begun to realize what these actually meant.

'Sir, I am faced with a life-altering decision. Which path should I choose?'

'My son, I am afraid I cannot tell you which path to choose, for it is the seeker to decide the path on his own, and only then does one choose the correct path.'

'But isn't a guru supposed to lead the way for his disciples?'

'I have told you earlier, Atul. A guru's role is like a catalyst in a chemical reaction. A catalyst is always hidden; to the onlooker, it appears as if the two chemicals have reacted and led to the creation of a third element. It is the love of a disciple that makes it seem that the guru has shown the way, but in reality it's you and your inner self that chooses the path.'

'What should I do now, Guruji? I have stabbed Priya in the back again. My actions will put her career in trouble.'

'But you have your career at stake too,' Ahmed Ali's voice said.

'Yes, but I am unable to choose one of the two.'

'Who said you have to choose one? You choose a path that takes you to love and builds your career.'

'Does such a path exist?'

'Very much and you have to create it.'

'How?'

'The path of truth, the path of acceptance, the path of surrender. When you walk on this path, you will have to search for your destination. And that destination, my son, will be your destination, your wisdom. It will not be knowledge that you have borrowed from someone else.'

'Walking on such a path will be painful.'

'Son, it is the toughest path that leads one to liberation. A true seeker walks on this path with complete understanding and awareness. Surrender will lead to the creation of a new you. But true surrender can happen only when every element inside you is ready for the aahuti (offering) in the sacred fire. This act will lead to prayashchit (repentance) and prayashchit is like getting burnt in the heat of the fire inside you.

'It is like a raw material, which when burnt in the furnace comes out shining. The shine in the metal is not unreal, it is real, and it belongs to the metal, nobody has given it that, it was inside the metal, the same world then starts looking at the metal with awe and beauty and is ready to pay any price to get the metal. So, it is your wish to choose a path of the metal ready to be burnt and come out shining or the other path, the foundation of which you have already laid. Remember, Atul, being human offers infinite possibilities for you to be what you want. You can go downwards or come upwards and shine, the choice is yours.'

~

There was a long silence. I felt immense pain and a burning sensation. The heat was all over me. I opened my eyes and looked around. My body was being burnt by the fierce rays of the sun.

Was I dreaming?

I got up, poured some water on my face. I had not changed my clothes from last evening. I did not feel like doing so today. It no longer mattered if I was wearing dirty clothes. I only wanted to be clean from inside.

Priya had a late afternoon flight—I had to talk to her before she left for Bangalore, so I drove towards Gurgaon. My phone's battery had conked off and I was unable to get through to her. I tucked the handset inside my jacket and drove as fast as the roads in NCR allowed me to.

Every single vehicle I crossed felt like a milestone. Though I was driving, I could only think of Priya and the moments we had shared that made for magical memories. After giving the keys of my car to a valet, I ran towards the reception of Crowne Plaza and asked for Priya.

'She checked out half an hour ago,' I was informed.

I borrowed a cell phone from the receptionist and dialled Priya's number.

'Hello.'

'Hi, Priya, it's me.'

'Hi, where have you been? Your mobile is switched off, I tried you a number of times. Is everything...'

'It's a long story. I am in Gurgaon, I want to meet you urgently. Where are you?' I cut her short.

'I am in office. You are tense. Is everything all right?'

'Listen, I need to talk to you in private. Can I come over to your office? Should we meet at the food court in the next twenty minutes?'

'I will be there.'

I reached the food court and ordered a coffee. I thought

it would freshen me up but as I took a few sips, my stomach that had only had alcohol for dinner the previous night, felt a jolt. As I kept the cup back on the table, I saw Priya coming straight towards me. She came and sat down opposite me.

'Tell me,' she smiled. I did not know where to start. I had so much to say. I slowly took Priya's diary out of my jacket and kept it on the table. She was surprised, embarrassed, angry.

'Where the hell did you get this from?'

'I took it from your desk last night.'

'Did you read it?'

'Yes.'

I looked at her. I thought she would scream at me; instead, she touched my hand gently.

'You know it all now. You are the first person, besides my mother, who has read this.' She lowered her head and said, 'Now you know how much I missed you all my life.'

I kept my hand on hers and said, 'I love you so much, Priya. I want to confess something today.' She was confused.

It was time to liberate myself. I had to choose the path of truth, the path of surrender, and this was not possible without burning in the fire of Priya's hatred. No longer was I worried about my future. I knew Priya would leave me after hearing what I had done, but I was prepared for the consequences of my actions.

For a second, as if time had stopped for me, my entire life revolved around meeting Priya in the train, Ramakant, Lovely and myself laughing and hugging each other, telling a lie for the first time in front of Shuklaji, getting fired by Mr Bhanot, making love to Priya, Priya rushing out of my house crying, living a drugged and high octane life in Delhi, flights, international travel, parties, conferences, the images zoomed in one after the other. I took a deep breath and told Priya that I had guessed her password, logged into her system and made changes in the final report of the SWAAN tender that were favourable to Wiretech Insys.

Stunned, she kept looking into my eyes as if she wanted this to be a lie. Unfortunately, it wasn't.

'How could you do that to me?' she shook her head in disgust. 'Every time I got drawn towards you, you used me. I can't believe I trusted you, you son of bitch.'

She got up from the chair. I did not have the moral strength to look at her.

'You...you...don't know what you have done to my career...' She broke down and ran back to her office. I felt her pain and her disillusionment. As I saw her running away from me, I knew this was the last I would see of Priya in my life.

Yet I wanted to be around her and apologize profusely. So I ran back towards her. It was Saturday and not many people were around at the D&Y office. I took an elevator and reached her floor. As soon as the elevator doors opened, I ran towards the reception.

'Can you call Miss Priya? I want to talk to her. My name is Atul Shukla.'

He rang up and after muttering 'Yes, sir' a few times, he asked me to go inside without making an entry in the register. I hurried towards Priya's seat. She was sitting in her cubicle. Varun was with her.

No exchange of pleasantries. Turns out she has told him too.

'Welcome, Mr Intruder, a very smart move indeed. You tried everything—wooing us, being friends with us and when all of it did not help, you decided to play with a multibillion dollar company's reputation and tampered with an internal report, breaching the security of the company.' I was only looking at Priya. She was in tears and was staring at the ceiling.

'You know what, Mr Smartass, I can get you and your company booked for conspiring against the D&Y group, breach of internal security and tampering of important client data,' Varun said as he moved towards me.

'A young corporate executive charged for corporate theft. Nice headlines it will make in the leading dailies, Mr Atul Shukla.' He paused for a second and continued, 'Milord, the offender should be given a very strict punishment, which should set a precedent in the corporate world and all the young guns joining should take a lesson from this.'

'I didn't know you could be so dramatic.' I only wanted to hear Priya's voice in this.

Varun came closer and pointed a finger towards my face. 'You certainly don't know what I can do.' I had not realized it but by this time almost five security guards had come behind me. Varun looked at them and said, 'Catch him, he is an unauthorized entry in our office. Ram Singh, you keep the back-up of last evening's camera recordings. He has fooled us and entered our office using our colleague's identity card, making a fake entry in the register. This will be important proof against him. Rawat, call for our security chief, he will get in touch with the police. Meanwhile, I will ask our legal counsel and corporate affairs officer to call his company's head office and send them a legal notice.'

Varun moved back after firing orders at his men. The security officers had grabbed my hands and started dragging me outside the D&Y office. For once I did not put up any resistance. I knew this would happen to me. I stopped and looked at Priya, 'I came back Priya, just to tell you that I love you, and will always love you.' A shocked and disappointed Priya kept staring into nothingness.

15

The Thug

THE GUARDS MADE me sit inside the meeting room in the reception. It was the same room where I had chanced upon Priya for the second time in my life. The difference was that back then I was a guest and now I was a thug.

I came as a thug then.

My mobile phone was still dead. Strangely, I was completely aloof to what was happening. No longer did it bother me that my career had crumbled into pieces. Neither was I affected by the fact that I may just be convicted. Would I still be worthy of employment once I came out of jail? How would my parents react? Amid this sea of life-altering questions, I should have been sad, unhappy, depressed. But I felt stronger, I felt as if I had attained a new level of enlightenment spiritually. Yes, life was about to change forever, but now I had the strength and the will to lead it with honour.

I sat in the room quietly for the next three hours. My eyes were shut and I could feel every breath that I was taking. Suddenly, I heard the sound of a door opening. Mitali Bagga came towards the reception. She was wearing a sweater and jeans, her short straight hair was untied. Mitali was accompanied by the security head of Wiretech Insys. Soon after, I saw Veerendra Singh coming out of the elevator. He was walking slowly, his eyes examining every part of the building while he was also searching for me. I stood up and walked towards the glass door.

Veeru saw me and asked, 'Tiger, *yeh kya naya hai?* What have you got yourself into?' He asked me to sit and then moved towards Mitali, who was standing at the reception and talking to the guard. She looked nervously at me, unsure of how to break the 'bad news'.

After some time, the police arrived. They were five, one senior officer and other sub-inspectors and constables. Mitali requested the guards to let her come inside the room.

'Hi, Mitali.' She put her hand on my cheek and said, 'I am not going to ask why you did it. But at least tell me your side of the story.'

'What's their side of the story?'

'That does not matter. You tell me yours.'

'Well, I did change the report on Priya's laptop and deliberately kept her occupied so that she did not notice the changes and sent the internal report to the client as it was.'

She shook her head in disgust. 'This is not as simple as it looks Atul. You also know the client is the government of Himachal Pradesh and an internationally reputed consultant like D&Y does not fuck around with clients' reports. They have a legal contract signed with the government and they are charging money. Shit!'

'What does Rajput say?' I was curious to know his view.

Perhaps this was the question Mitali dreaded answering.

'He has spoken to the India MD and has sent a mail to our global business practice head claiming that he did not have any idea what you were about to do and that he never asked you to do anything of this sort. Based on the police complaint that D&Y has filed, the global business practice has asked me...to... fire you immediately.' She paused and looked at me.

Sushil has turned his back on me. Why am I not surprised! Just a day before he had asked me to get the work done by hook or by crook, and now he was pretending to be a holy cow in front of his seniors and distancing himself from me. I didn't care if Sushil stood by me or not; after all, this was my redemption.

Veeru was asking for the guards' permission to let him come inside the room. The guards agreed. As soon as Veeru entered, I hugged him and broke down. His eyes were also filled with tears. Though we did not talk, it was evident that somewhere Veeru was proud of what I had done.

'*Arrey*, Tiger, *yeh duniya saali kutti hai, par tu to sher hai* (This world is dog but you are a tiger). We will leave everything and go to my village in UP. We will do farming there. Both of us will wear long boots, cowboy hats, smoke cigars with jazz music playing in the background. That will be LIFE, my friend. We will live like *kings*. Fuck them all.' Veeru was trying his best to sound funny in an attempt to underplay the seriousness of the situation.

'Sure, we will.'

'What else?' I turned towards Mitali.

'Wiretech Insys will be issuing an official apology letter to D&Y, informing them of the action taken against you, and then it's up to the law and D&Y what they do to you,' Mitali's low voice completed the sentence. She was like a slayer who had the dirty job of executing the fugitive.

The senior of the five policemen, who was the Station Head Officer (SHO), asked me to come out of the room. As I began to comply, Veeru began to assure me. 'Tiger, don't worry. Tomorrow is Sunday and the courts are closed. I will get you out of this mess soon.' He then came closer and whispered, *'Tu bole to Rajput ki supari de doon.'* I touched Veeru's hand, smiled and said, 'Not required, Thakur sahib.'

I waved goodbye to Mitali. I knew her official responsibility would compel her to send the firing letter to my permanent address in hard copy, thereby informing my parents that their son's Big Corporate Dream had finally fallen apart. Mitali hugged me and said, 'Take care.'

As I went outside the room, one of the sub-inspectors held my hands and put them in handcuffs. As we were leaving the D&Y building, my eyes were desperately searching for Priya. She was nowhere to be seen.

16

Beginning of the End Continues...

23 December 2012
6.50 a.m.

The chill in the air hits again. I wake up and rub my eyes. The old man is still sleeping in one corner of the cell. I hold my feet with my hands in a desperate attempt to keep them warm. I had been revisiting my life all of last night and did not realize when I had fallen asleep. My parents are yet to know about the recent developments. I wonder what my father will think of me. Will he be proud of what I did? Or will he be flabbergasted by the extent to which I could go to fulfil my goals? Will he and my mother come for me?

My thoughts are cut short by Shamsher Singh. 'Have some tea,' he says, offering me a cup of piping hot tea. I do not refuse this time. After finishing it, I feel a certain heaviness in my eyes; I can sense that my body is completely exhausted. I do not remember clearly when I pass out.

1.40 P.M.

Shamsher Singh wakes me up. This time he offers me a plate of rajma chawal. I gobble that quickly and go back to sleep.

5.30 P.M.

I look at my watch. I have been sleeping for nearly 11 hours with small eating breaks in between. My mouth stinks. My body is full of aches. My bottom has become stiff. It feels as if I have been in this cell for years.

How strange to feel liberated in this dark, dingy space!

'Shamsher Singhji.'

'Yes?' he turns around.

'Can I please get a notebook and a pen?' Shamsher Singh looks at me with a squinted eye and nods his head. He moves slowly from his seat and after ten minutes, he hands me a pen and a brand new notebook he has got from a nearby shop.

'Thank you, sir.'

His face remains expressionless.

5.40 P.M.

I sit down and start writing something, something very dear to me, something I have learnt in life. The story of my life as told through just six evenings.

24 DECEMBER 2010

6.00 A.M.

I have been writing for the whole night. It's a foggy morning today. For a moment, my heart goes out to business travellers who must be taking early morning flights and are cursing the fog for delaying their plans.

Not so long ago, I used to be one of them.

Shamsher Singh once again offers a comforting cup of hot tea. As soon as I am done with it, I ask Shamsher if I could relieve my body of the unwanted fluids. He allows me to do so. Sleep evades me. I am full of energy; I am more awake now than ever.

1.45 P.M.

It's past noon now. I have immersed myself in the notebook. Shamsher Singh offers me some food. I feel I am being treated marginally better than some of the other inmates. Shamsher's inquisitive mind is perhaps wondering, *Doesn't this boy want to go home? Is he enjoying writing inside this cell?*

6.10 P.M.

It's quite dark outside. Shamsher bangs his stick on the iron grills of the cell.

'Chhore,' he addresses me, and asks me to get up. I stand up slowly, my body now indifferent to the pain. He leads me to his superior. As I move, I see Veeru sitting in front of the SHO with a lawyer and, as usual, he has managed to chat up the SHO. He looks at me and smiles. I walk towards them, Veeru comes and hugs me. I hold him tightly.

'You came,' I tell him as my eyes well up with tears.

'I had to,' Veeru replies.

'*Hum bhi hai rahon main.*' The voice seems familiar to me. I look back to find Ramakant Murthy standing near the entrance of the police station.

'Rama…' I look at Veeru who is smiling. I run towards my old friend and hug him. I notice that he has shaved off his moustache and is now looking lean, fair and fit.

'How the hell are you here?' Words are barely coming out of my heavy throat.

'For you.'

'Fuck you, no more philosophy.' I punch him on the belly.

'After I made some money in my consultancy business, I came to India almost a year ago and started working with Guruji for his NGO near Jamshedpur.'

'Why the fuck did you not call me then?'

'My mistake. After I landed in India, I got so busy establishing the school and the NGO that I just couldn't call you. Guruji told me last night to go to Delhi immediately and meet you. Your number was not reachable. I contacted your office, and they led me to your HR lady, who gave me Veerendra's number and so here I am.' He spread his arms in the air, and we hugged each other once again. I did not ask why Guruji had told him to come to Delhi. I knew the answer.

'If your *Bharat milap* is over, can we do some work?' Veeru says. We both look at him and laugh. As the documents are handed over to me, I realize that these are not bail documents. I ask Veeru about my bail.

'Priya has requested her company not to file a case against you and she has taken the entire responsibility of the goof-up on herself. D&Y has, in turn, written to the government of Himachal Pradesh acknowledging the error as a typing error from the employee and assured them of taking action against the said employee. Priya has resigned from D&Y on moral grounds.'

She sacrificed her career for a man who had betrayed her. Almost.

'Where is she now?' I ask Veeru.

'I am afraid she left.'

My broken heart and body are unable to think.

'Mitali has met the global heads of Wiretech Insys and has insisted that they should not fire you. Instead, you will have to give a resignation letter to the company,' Veeru informs me.

Being fired would have been the end of the road for me in the corporate world.

'What about Sushil?'

'Sushil is busy telling everyone that he could not believe Atul Shukla could be such an unethical person and that he is happy that the small piece of shit that could have harmed the whole company has been thrown out. Atul, I have also put in my papers,' Veeru looks into my eyes while saying this.

Surprised, I look at Veeru, demanding an explanation for why he has put his career at stake.

'I could not take this shit from Sushil or anyone for that matter. On the evening of your arrest, Sushil called an emergency meeting and was throwing his usual nonsense about "corporate ethics" everywhere. I listened to him quietly. When he finished, I stayed back late at work and spared a thought for everything that was happening. I thought about you, your commitment and sacrifice. I realized that for so many years I had been working with these people like a coward, knowing fully well what they were doing in the company. I realized that being true does not only mean you should be true to yourself, it also means accepting truth as a way of life. My job should not be more important than what I stand for in my life.'

'I wrote an email to the global compliance office of Wiretech Insys, telling him about the "understanding" and "structuring" that Sushil along with his bosses in India were doing through his team. He replied immediately, asking me to join a private video conference with him. I told him each and everything about the way the India business was being run. The global management of Wiretech Insys has sent a team to India to audit all the emails, documents, invoices and is questioning Sushil along with everyone involved in all the big deals. I am serving my notice period with the company now. Sushil did face me once in the office, but he did not say anything to me. His eyes were enough to tell me how much he hated me.'

I hugged Veeru and wanted to thank him for everything he had done, but I could not bring myself to say anything.

25 December 2012

We are driving down to the outskirts of Jamshedpur. There is a certain serenity in the winter sunshine; it has the most calming effect. It is inspiring me to keep scribbling in the notebook.

'What are you writing?' asks Ramakant.

'It's about six evenings in my life,' I smile.

'Are you writing a book?' Ramakant gives me a confused look.

'Maybe,' I chuckle.

Guruji's NGO ashram is nearly 10 kilometres from the hustle bustle of the town. We enter the main gate; the campus is spread across five acres of land and is surrounded by lush green fields and trees. The main building is white, single-storeyed and square-shaped. It has four rooms with an open space connecting them with each other. Ramakant tells me the four square rooms represent the four elements—earth, water, fire and air—and the décor of each of these rooms has been done to match the elements they represent. The open space between these rooms is a symbol of life.

Guruji lives in this building. The first room towards the left is the office of the ashram, the other rooms include a library, a classroom and a restroom. Ramakant and his childhood friends who had once formed the 'Friends Club' are now well settled and have pooled in money and resources to fund this NGO. They have registered themselves as the 'Friends Welfare Society'. The society runs this NGO and they have also opened a school for underprivileged children.

Ramakant and I wait outside the room where Guruji is taking a class. Apparently, a bunch of children have come to get their 'doubts' cleared by Sir. All of them are from different age groups. They are solving their textbook sums and discussing the solutions one by one with Sir. Guruji's method of teaching marries scientific concepts with spiritual understanding. As I peek into the classroom, I cannot help but see a Ramakant Murthy in each child. These students do not have to pay any fee.

Lucky rascals! They are getting to understand this world so early in life.

After the 'class' is over, we enter the room. I look at Guruji, sitting humbly in a chair, reading the papers his students have left. A small decorated Christmas tree is standing in one corner of the room. It's been almost eight years since I met him. He still looks the same, though he is a lot weaker now. I kneel down to touch his feet. He looks at me and then hugs me. Tears are flowing endlessly from my eyes. For me, Guruji indeed proved to be a catalyst of change. I may have lost a lot in life, but I feel privileged. I cannot see the path ahead of me, but I know my destination.

'Guruji, much has happened to me in life, and I have learnt

a lot from it. But there is still a bit of blockage. Help me get through this,' I ask him. Ramakant looks at me and smiles. He marvels at my use of such philosophical words.

'As I said earlier, Atul, every child is born talented and so are you. You are drawn to positive and negative energies in equal measure. You could not score well in your academics and hence a negative blockage kept building inside you. As that blockage grew, so did your desire to prove your worth to the world. You wanted to have an illustrious career in a big company, earning more money, reaching newer highs and showing the world that you were no loser. This blockage turned you into an unethical person, who did not hesitate to lie or manipulate people at the drop of a hat. But little did you know we are all ruled by our karma.'

'Your penchant for lying and deceiving people had nothing to do with the nature of your work. Regardless of your work, imbibing honesty and truthfulness in your work, love and relationships is a virtue many deem negotiable. The path to greatness is simple, there is nothing great about it.'

I listen to each word coming out of Guruji's mouth with the curiosity of a child.

'I have lost Priya.'

'Do you miss her?'

'Forever and ever,' my eyes well up with tears.

'Atul.' The voice sounds familiar. It is Priya's. My heart begins to beat faster and as I look outside I see Priya standing there. She is wrapped in a woollen jacket; her face is as charming as ever. She looks at me and, at once, both our cheeks turn moist with tears.

I take fast steps towards her. She, too, does not care about the world and runs towards me and we hug each other. Both of us are enfolded in each other's warmth. We are crying and laughing at the same time. For the first time ever in our lives, both of us have accepted love for each other and are not afraid to tell the world. Three nights ago, I had confessed to my wrongdoing to protect her career and now she has given it up to prevent me from serving a sentence in prison. No longer do we live in the past; we're living in the moment and we are living each moment.

'Why did you do this? You should have let me rot.'

'You took a brave and honest step, Atul, and had it not been true love for me, you would not have done this.'

We hug each other again and it is only when Ramakant comes out of the classroom that we realize there are other people around us. I look at him, he knows he has to answer my questions.

'Guruji spoke to Priya and gave her the courage to come to you.'

Holding each other's hands, Priya and I walk towards the room where he is sitting.

Priya folds her hand and says a soft namaste to Guruji.

'God bless you, kid. You are a brave girl. It's not just Atul who has graduated to a new level of understanding. Forgiveness is the most generous form of giving. Atul's surrender and sacrifice were perfectly matched by your forgiveness and sacrifice. Surrender is the beginning of acceptance. It takes a lot of courage to defy the norms that the world has created to accept each other. May the One always be with you.'

Priya and I stare at Guruji and then look straight into each other's eyes.

'What will you do now, Atul and Priya? Both of you have sacrificed whatever you had earned and strived for all your life just to be with each other,' Guruji asks.

He knows the answer but wants to hear it from us.

'Guruji, I will quote a story from the Vishnu Purana. After the death of his wife Sati, Shiva is in immense pain and is destroying everything. The Devas are worried and they pray to Shiva to stop for the greater good of humanity. Shiva realizes this and he responds by closing his eyes, and begins to understand that it is his mind which is filled with memories, desires and ego that have led him to pain, suffering and misery. It is only when Shiva destroys his mind and ego with tapa and yoga that he achieves consciousness. There is no confusion then, only clarity. Both of us have gone through a similar phase. Our sacrifice and forgiveness is our tapa,' Priya concludes.

'That's impressive,' says Ramakant, '*Beta* Atul, *tu to gaya* (You are gone)!'

I did not read this in her diary.

'Atul, there is one more debt that you have to pay,' says Ramakant.

'Debt? Whose?'

'I have dialled Lovely Chaddha's number. Speak to him,' he hands over his mobile phone to me. Shocked, I look towards Priya, who insists I talk to Lovely.

'*Tussi kaise ho, paaji,*' Lovely's voice is as playful as ever.

'Lovely…' I say slowly. There is silence on the other side.

'I am sorry, Lovely. I am in Jamshedpur with Ramakant and Ahmed Ali, Priya is also with me. Priya and I have decided to marry. *Bol* date *kab ki* decide *karen?*' My throat becomes heavy as I say the words. This is the first time that I have publicly acknowledged my relationship with Priya.

Still no response from the other end of the line.

'I am really sorry, Lovely. Please forgive me.'

'Oye bainchod, you took so much of time to say such a small thing,' Lovely's voice is cracking, he is in tears as well. 'You decide any time, I will come wherever and whenever you call me.'

We chat for some more time. Years of being away from each other's lives hasn't robbed our conversation of intimacy. The pauses overlap the start of another sentence. We update each other on our lives. Lovely tells me he is well settled in Jalandhar and owns an electronics service centre in the area. He has a team of ten engineers under him. He is married now and has a two-year-old daughter, Loveleen.'

I end the conversation and give the phone to Ramakant.

'Thanks, Rama.'

Ramakant's infectious smile is back on his face. 'These are his blessings,' he says. For once, I understand what he means by 'his'. Before Priya and I leave the ashram premises, we touch Guruji's feet again. He places his hand on our heads and says, 'Ath yog sadhnam (It begins now).'

As we step out, I have a firmer grip on Priya's hand. It's dark now, a long day is finally coming to an end. For Priya and I, though, it is the dawn of a lifetime of togetherness.

Acknowledgements:

Acknowledgements are usually a boring read (except for the ones who are being acknowledged by the writer!). Yet for me, this is the most important part of my novel, for during this five-minute read I salute those individuals who are an integral part of my life and this project. Needless to say, without their support I would not have completed my first endeavour in something which I am passionate about.

First and foremost, I thank the two most lovely ladies in my life, my wife Vrinda and my daughter Tanvie. One of them was a pillar of support during the entire writing process of five years, and other gave me inspiration to write.

I would also like to thank my parents, for blessing me with their unconditional love; and my elder brother Piyush Dixit. His one word of advice changed me from the person who I was to the one I am now.

I also would also like to thank Swati Chauhan for being kind enough to share two of her most wonderful poems 'You & I' and 'Lonely Heart' without which Priya's Diary would not have been complete; Kusum Wahi, for her childlike enthusiasm about the project and her superb dedication in helping me proofread the book; Anamika Chatterjee for her exceptional editing; my friends Vishwanath Saxena, Jhimli, Rimi Das and Rahul Tandon, for their patience in going through various drafts of the book; Veena Dubey for all the amazing images in the book; and my brothers Ranu, Anu, Manu, and Sanu, for being there and backing me in whatever I do. I would also like to thank the editorial team at Rupa Publications, without whom this book would not have been a reality.

As they say, a life without friendship is not worth living: so I dedicate this book to all my friends without whom I could never have done this!

I would like to end with this verse of Kabir:

'*Guru, Govind* dono khade, *Kaake lagoon pao;*
Balihari Guru aapke; Govind Diyo Batae.
(Master and God both are in front of me, to who should I bow,
I bow to you O' master, who showed me the way of God!)'